DRAGON CALLED

CASSIE ALEXANDER

KARA LOCKHARTE

Copyright © 2020 by Erin Cashier and Kara Lockharte

Cover design by the Bookbrander

All rights reserved.

Note: This book is a work of fiction. No part of this book may be reproduced in any form or by any electronic or mechanical means, including information storage and retrieval systems, without written permission from the author, except for the use of brief quotations in a book review.

About the Author

On her own, Cassie's a nurse by day and writer by night, living in the Bay Area with her husband, two cats, inside a massive succulent garden.

Whereas Kara's a California transplant by way of NYC and is still, to this day, searching for the perfect bagel (although the no-snow and strawberries out here help to make up for it.)

Follow Cassie on her newsletter for behind the scenes access at http://www.cassiealexander.com/newsletter or check out her website, www.cassiealexander.com

Follow Kara on Facebook, www.facebook.com/karalockharte or get a free book at her website, www.karalockharte.com/signup

To Clarion West 2007 and all the Clarion West Classes!

ABOUT DRAGON CALLED

Andie Ngo hasn't met a bad decision she won't make, but this one might turn out to be the best bad decision of her life.

Desperate for money after her deadbeat brother left her holding the bill for his bail bond, night nurse Andi agrees to take on a mysterious one-time nursing gig. When she finds out her employer is ruthless billionaire and all around asshole Damian Blackwood, she's determined to get the job done and get out as quickly as possible.

But nothing is as it seems, when a monster attacks and she is saved by an honest-to-god dragon. A golden scaled, sixty foot long, violent dragon...who is clearly Damian's other half. Her world is spun sideways but she can't forget the way he looked at her, like coveted treasure he's desperate to steal away for his hoard. The way he reacted when she discovered his secret. The way that when he was human again he...asked her for a date.

Fierce and independent Andi doesn't trust easily. The expensive suits, fancy cars, and spooky castle can't hide the truth: Damian is extremely dangerous, not to mention a monstrous beast.

She should say no. But what if she says yes?

CHAPTER ONE

While waiting for the bus, Andrea Ngo—Andi—had plenty of time to consider that answering an Overnight Help Wanted ad online may not have been the world's best idea. But it wasn't like her student loans were going to pay themselves; she was already working nights at the county hospital—and then there was the whole thing with her idiot brother's bail. Danny had gotten into stupid situations before, but she never thought he'd run out on her, miss his court date, and leave her stuck with a ten-thousand-dollar bail bond.

So, what was another shift or two? Who needed sleep anyhow? Sleep was definitely overrated. She took a pair of thick black plastic framed glasses out of her coat pocket and put them on. She had perfect vision, but she knew from experience glasses on Asian girls made people think she was either super smart or super sheltered—both of which had worked in her favor before.

The bus came, picked her up, and deposited her as far as it would go across town, at the bus stop outside the Briars Country Club. Its ominously-thorned, wrought iron gate made her glad she knew when her last tetanus shot was. She pulled out her phone to text the mysterious number that said she'd gotten the job in the first place.

I'm here, she texted. Five minutes early, no less. She took off her glasses, which turned out to be quite dirty from underuse and fogged them with her breath to wipe them down. She'd never been this close to the BCC before—there was never any point when she was most definitely not, nor would ever be, a member.

But working at her glasses stopped her from staring at her phone. The person who'd given her the number when she'd gotten the job had claimed to be Damian Blackwood's secretary. Andi found that hard to believe. What on earth would Damian Blackwood need a private nurse for one night for? Or—perhaps the better question—for whom?

She'd talked to an ambulance transport nurse once who'd gotten paid for an entire day to follow around a Saudi prince in his rig. So she might be getting paid just to watch someone breathe, barring an assassination attempt, which sounded lucrative and exciting.

But she'd never get to tell anyone about it—not even her roommate Sammy—because they'd made her sign a nondisclosure agreement. And then the text that had told her when to be here had made it clear that this assignment was "no questions asked."

Which would be hard because questions were like, *her thing*. Had to be. Because secrets could kill you—asking questions saved lives.

Andi ran an aggressive thumbnail over the glasses left lens, trying to scrape off a streak, and found a scratch too deep to ignore. She should've tried these on at home and brought one of her other half-dozen pairs. She sighed and pocketed them, returning to her phone to check the time.

And now *they*—whoever *they* were—were late.

Maybe this was all just an elaborate hoax. She crossed her arms in the dark, turning her back on the gates and the mansions behind them. She hated thinking like that because she knew the slightly paranoid anxiety that made her an excellent nurse was a double-edged sword when it came to life-coping skills.

But it'd stopped her from getting into the Subaru STI that Danny'd "borrowed" from a friend the last time she'd seen him—which stopped her from getting her prints in his freshly stolen car.

Andi checked the time again then jumped as the heavy gates behind her began to fold in on themselves, thorns disappearing like at the end of *Sleeping Beauty*. An all-black car—in a make she didn't recognize—pulled up. But she realized it was for her as it parked and a driver in a suit emerged.

He was…breathtaking. A Caucasian man with black hair, strong nose and chin, full lips, and piercing light brown eyes that appeared almost golden. The crisp black suit made him look sharp, but he didn't need it—which led to thinking about what he might look like without it, which was not appropriate right now, but Andi couldn't help herself. He was injuriously handsome—the kind of hot you'd do a double take for and wind up getting hit by an oncoming bus you hadn't noticed—and hot enough that there was no way he didn't know it. She more than knew his type, and she steeled herself to give him no response.

"Miss Ngo?" he asked as he opened the passenger door for her.

He actually pronounced her last name right, which was also sexy as hell. "Just Andi," she corrected him, getting into the back seat and scooting over. He took a moment to stare at her, and she felt a low-hipped thump of desire, which she concealed with a tight smile.

"Of course," he agreed, giving her a slight nod and a much warmer smile as he closed her door. He took the driver's seat again and looped the black car around to pull back behind the gates of the Briars like a tide.

She had no idea what kind of car she was in, but she had a feeling that Danny would lust for it. The interior leather felt buttery, and the drive was certainly a lot smoother than the city bus.

Too bad the whole "having a driver" thing made her uncomfortable. Admittedly, she couldn't drive, so she really did need one, but her last boyfriend hadn't even opened her door for her on their first date. And Josh had definitely not looked like *that*.

Andi-girl, you need to have fun and get out more. She could hear Eumie gently chastising her in her head, and right after that, her roommate Sammy, adding, *And you need to get laid.*

She was willing to admit that both those things might be true—but nothing like that would happen tonight.

"So, we're going to Blackwood's estate?" she asked the driver, trying to make innocent conversation as the car rose in the hills. She glanced up at the rearview—waiting for him to respond—and realized the defiant blue streak in her black hair was showing. *Shit, shit, shit* – she hadn't gotten into nurse mode yet, but it was time. Her hands reached up and wound her hair into a practiced bun that hid the color.

"We are indeed," said the driver, not taking his eyes off the road.

"Do you know who I'll be taking care of?"

This made him look back at her in the rear view, brow lifted in bemusement. "Someone who needs your help—clearly."

Andi groaned on the inside. "That's a little vague."

"Would you prefer to hear that I'm not at liberty to say?" His tone was clearly teasing.

"No, not really." Andi rolled her eyes. Once again, hot did not equal charming. "So, what's he like?"

"Who?" the driver asked, overly oblivious.

"You know who; come on," she said, leaning forward in the car to talk to him between the front seats. "Damian."

She'd googled him, obviously, but that hadn't told her much. The Blackwoods were old money, rode over on the Mayflower-style: stocks, yachts, islands. But it seemed like no one had taken a picture of the man since he turned thirty—twenty years ago.

"And what makes you think he'd be involved with the hiring of temporary staff?" the driver asked, twisting to smirk back at her.

So much for blue-collar solidarity. Andi sank back into her seat and loosened her scarf. "Right. So, is there anything you can tell me about this gig? Or do you just do as he says, 'no questions asked'?" she said in a tone of voice that mocked the text she'd gotten.

"Hmmm. Asking too many questions of the Blackwoods is generally a bad policy," he said in a cautionary tone. "Or of anyone, really."

"Too bad that's like half my job," Andi muttered beneath her breath, then more loudly said, "No questions, huh? Sounds like a great person to work for."

The car took a swooping right turn. "Just do what you're told, and you'll be fine."

"Yes, of course," she clipped. Good help didn't gossip—and that was all she'd be. She wasn't getting paid to be curious. The driver swung left without turning on his turn signal, and she swayed with the car.

The road rose as it curved, zigging and zagging up the side of a hill. She twisted to look behind her and caught a view of the city below, all lit up like a rippled sheet of gold. It was so unexpectedly beautiful she gasped—and then it felt like she'd been stabbed. In her chest. Right below her heart. She pressed a hand beneath her breast, trying to figure out what was wrong with her and if she should confide it to this strange man, but then the pain was combined with the strange impression that she should run back down to the city lights below where she knew that she'd be safe—from *what, though?* —*as* prickling terror rushed over her entire body like ice cold water.

"Are you all right?" the driver asked, glancing back at her in the rearview, his voice serious for the first time since she'd met him.

"Yes," she said defiantly, even though she still felt like she was being stabbed—by fear itself. Her heart was hammering so fast, like the time she'd been chased by the cops because of her dumb brother or the time she'd been mugged—but she'd never felt such an intense urge to *run-run-run*.

Why?

She double-blinked and forced herself to breathe, looking out the window at the city's golden streetlight tapestry. It swept out like wings to encompass the hills on both sides, and from somewhere in the depths of her childhood memories, her Auntie Kim's voice burbled up: *There are dragons in this world.*

"Miss Ngo?" There was a note of concern in the driver's voice that hadn't been there earlier.

Why on earth did she think about Grand Auntie Kim? It had been years since she'd seen the old woman who had taken care of her as a child during the summer, who'd told her and Danny stories of dragons after their dad had walked out on them and their mother had had to work. Andi inhaled deeply and shook her head. *Whatever this is, you are bigger than it. You have handled worse. You're going to be fine.*

Or, said a darker part of her mind, *you're having a heart attack at a freakishly young age, and in about three seconds, you should ask Mr. Handsome here to call 911.*

"Andi?" the driver pressed.

"Do you know CPR?" Andi asked, half-joking, half-not—then the sense of terror lifted just as fast as it'd come on. "Oh my God," she whispered to herself, sinking back into the car's luxury leather interior. "Okay. Never mind. I'm fine. Honest."

His eyes narrowed at her in the rearview. A flash of anger? That was on him, not her.

"Don't worry," he growled, suddenly a much darker man. "You're allowed to be here."

What an odd turn of phrase.

She would've asked him why he'd said it quite like that, but she was too happy to not feel like she was dying anymore. The car swung around again, and the pavement turned to cobblestones as they pulled through a final gate.

The driver slowed and parked in the roundabout, right in front of the mansion's huge church-like doors, and she quickly got out to breathe fresh air before he could come around and release her. She leaned against the car and looked up.

Compared to any place Andi'd ever lived—or ever seen—the house was utterly ridiculous. It wasn't a house so much as a castle, and it had the kind of turrets that you expected to see archers peeking out from—although, in this day and age, and with Blackwood-level money, machine guns seemed more apt. Stained glass windows dotted the upper floors, some glowing with light, while ivy grew aggressively up the lower ones, crawling out of a garden that could best be described as feral. A huge circular fountain behind her had a dragon head on top of it shooting out water instead of smoke.

The driver walked around her and opened the front door, and light beamed from somewhere inside as he gestured for her. "Ready?"

Andi forced a lightness she didn't feel into her voice and expression, plastering on a smile so sweet it was giving her cavities. "As I'll ever be!"

SWALLOWING FOR STRENGTH, she walked behind him indoors. They were together in a vast entryway that had three sets of stairs, wide ones arching toward the right and left wings of the house, and an odd spiral staircase that shot straight up. Her eyes followed it to a circular door in the ceiling, two floors up. A belfry? Some kind of service hatch? Her guesses were interrupted by the driver reaching for her, and she stepped back quickly without thinking. "I-I didn't catch your name?"

"It doesn't matter," he said.

She stared at his open hand and then looked to him. The corners of his lips were turned upward, teasing her, and it felt like her heart stopped beating for a moment. *Dammit.* Was he taunting or flirting with her? Was he so hot he just assumed he'd get his way? Or was he so used to hanging out with rich people he thought he was one, just like when clerks were rude to you for no reason in fancy stores?

He cleared his throat and lifted his hand slightly. "Would you like me to take your coat, or do you prefer to wear it while nursing?"

She had a sudden urge to meet him late at night in a pool hall and see how much she could take him for, but she took off her coat and handed it over. "You're assuming I'll get the job."

He shrugged. "I'm assuming you're competent. But I've been wrong before."

"Thanks for the vote of confidence, Mr. It-Doesn't-Matter," she said. Why wouldn't he give her his name? Her roommate Sammy was convinced that answering an 'Overnight Help Wanted' ad online was Andi's beginning of a true-life crime show on Investigation Discovery—and maybe she was right. Maybe Mr. No-Name was a felon or something? Something he'd have in common with Danny if she couldn't talk her Uncle Lee into getting her brother an expensive lawyer. She squinted at the driver. His reluctance to tell her his name only made her want to know more.

He resisted her dig. "And your phone?" he asked. She handed it over, much more reluctantly. "You did sign an NDA," he reminded her, as he put it in his pocket.

"But what if there's an emergency?"

"We'll give you a spare."

A spare phone wasn't the same thing as *her* phone, but she tried to shake it off.

He glanced at his watch, and his expression became serious. "If you'll follow me," he said, and then started walking without looking back to make sure she did so. She almost had to trot after him. He was so much taller than she was—at least six-three to her five-nothing—and he was apparently in a hurry. Then again, maybe she was relieving someone else—another hired hand—who needed to leave quickly.

At least chasing after him let her see his ass. His suit was particularly well cut around him, not leaving much to the imagination—not when your imagination was as good as hers. He surprised her by stopping and turning back around, as though he'd known she was looking. She stopped, too, like they were playing a game of red-light green-light.

"Coming?" he asked, waving her up.

"I'm trying to, sheesh," she said, striding forward, almost out of breath.

"Come a little faster, then," he encouraged her. His eyes narrowed briefly, and she knew he knew exactly what he'd said to her as he turned back around. She wasn't sure if she should be irritated or ever-so-slightly pleased—her brain said the first, while her body said the latter.

Shut up, body. Andi always ended up falling for the broken, temperamental types. There was something alluring about trying to fix things—and people. But she knew better now, after several exes, and tried to get all of that out at work, where people actually *did* need fixing.

They practically raced through a living room, appointed with a mix of plush couches in old and modern styles, statuary of all kinds, two fireplaces on either end big enough to roast a bear in, and vases filled with flowers almost halfway to the cavernous ceiling. Past that was a dining room with a table elaborately set, too many chandeliers to count, and a long hall with many locked doors. She could tell they were locked because they were bolted from the outside—some with more than one bolt and the locks were exaggerated, even comical—like they were meant for the outside of pirate chests. She couldn't help herself; she stopped in front of the last locked door and inhaled, a question on her lips.

"Mmm, mmm," he said with a closed mouth, mockingly as if she were a naughty child, then he had the nerve to turn and wink at her. "No questions, remember?"

Andi's jaw clenched. She was *so* going to find out his name. But he started walking again without waiting for her—until they reached a final door.

"You're late," said a voice from inside the room. Damian himself? She straightened her shoulders and walked in.

No. The man who'd spoken was far too young to be Damian. While Mr. No-Name was so attractive as to almost be otherworldly, this new man was the pride of the Midwest, a golden boy through and through. Hair the color of rust, lightly tanned skin, and a build that said he could pick a girl—or several—up.

"Sorry. Someone didn't open the gates." Mr. No-Name's voice was almost acidic, and Andi realized that this is who he'd been mad at in the car, not her. But why? All the gates she'd seen had opened.

It didn't really matter though, because just past the homecoming king, Andi could finally see why she'd been brought here.

She could tell the room had once been a library, even though the shelves were mostly clear, and the only thing remaining to hint at its prior function were leather couches pushed to the side and the scent of old books. Now though, the place where the couches had surely been was occupied by a man in a hospital bed, surrounded by the accoutrements of the sick and infirm—oxygen tanks, monitors, IV pumps on IV poles, a chest tube, a feeding pump spinning like a spindle, and, impossibly out of place for her nursing experience thus far, a small Siamese cat lay curled at the end of the bed.

"I was a little busy," the other man defended himself, gesturing at the bedridden man. Apparently, no one was concerned about the cat.

Mr. No-Name opened his mouth to say something, and Andi cut him off. "Well, I'm here now." She walked up to the bed, blinking in the dim light. She thought she recognized him, from grainy newspaper photos. "Is this…Mr. Blackwood?" It looked like him. A little.

Mr. No-Name came to stand beside her. "It doesn't matter who he is. Can you keep him alive for eight hours?"

She tilted her head to look up at him. "Maybe—if you tell me what's wrong with him, first." What she could see of him was covered in splotchy bruises. There was an oxygen mask on his face, and Andi belatedly realized his tightly-restrained arms were both insanely muscled and covered in tattoos.

Definitely not Mr. Blackwood then—unless Mr. Blackwood was even more interesting than she'd assumed.

"He fell down the stairs," said Mr. Midwest entirely unconvincingly. Andi looked over at him to ask for more information and caught him looking over her at Mr. No-Name, his face full of concern.

"He's starting to wake up. I don't want the first face he sees to be a stranger."

"Grimalkin's here," Mr. No-Name said, with a pointed look at the cat, and then he jerked his head toward the door. "I need you out with me tonight. You know why." He held up a wrist and tapped on a watch that probably cost as much as the car he'd driven her in.

Drivers definitely didn't make that kind of money.

Mr. No-Name-Driver-With-a-Fancy-Watch.

Andi stopped herself from making a discomfited sound. She already knew from painful personal experience that rich people played weird games, and if it was more likely she'd get this job by pretending to be dumb, fine. It was only for one night, after all. The sooner she started working, the sooner she could make Danny's bail, and then maybe all this would make sense—an emphasis on the maybe. "Look—can somebody here just give me a report?"

The man she was replacing dragged his gaze away from Mr. No-Name and started talking to her. At her, really.

She pulled out a pen and paper and wrote everything down, asking appropriate questions at appropriate times, but she couldn't shake the feeling that she was being partially shouted at and definitely judged. When he was through, she held up a hand. "Three things."

"Go," he allowed her.

"The cat?" She couldn't help but ask.

The driver answered her. "He's practically a family member. Presence nonnegotiable. Next?"

"Okay, then." *Weird-ass rich people.* Andi shrugged and looked back at the patient. "So, why is he here? Why not a hospital?"

"In the city?" Mr. Midwest was incredulous.

"Yeah. Why not? There're good hospitals there."

"Hospitals aren't safe," Mr. Midwest stated—like that was a known fact.

Andi bit her lips, hard, to not say anything about his bizarre opinions. "All right, then," she went on. "Third is, who are you? Medically, I mean."

"His name's Austin; he used to be a paramedic," Mr. No-Name said for the man.

"And in the Marines," Austin added.

She stuck her hand out, so Austin would have to shake it. "I'm Andi."

"Ah. An Andi, not Andy," Austin said, with slightly different emphasis, giving Mr. No-Name a glare.

"It's not my fault your assumptions were sexist," Mr. No-Name said, a slight grin flickering at the corner of his mouth. He looked meaningfully at his watch again, and Austin disappeared down a hall. "So. Eight hours?" Mr. No-Name asked her.

From Austin's report, this patient mostly sounded like a wait-and-see. He was injured and unconscious, but there was no real reason he hadn't woken up yet—other than possible brain damage. Which, yeah, made this whole level of secrecy, perhaps understandable? If you were the head of a household worth a fortune and someone got injured on your watch, you might need to keep their issues under wraps. She glanced at the patient's vitals on the monitor, the level of urine in the foley, and the slowly draining chest tube. She could keep almost anyone alive for eight hours—at the hospital. But what would happen here if things went poorly? This situation was bizarre, and even though they were paying her a ton, she still had her license to think of. She glanced up and found Mr. No-Name watching her shamelessly—so shamelessly, she flushed.

Austin reappeared, pushing a crash cart before she could stutter out any words. "You know what to do with this?"

"Of course." The presence of a crash cart allayed only some of her fears. "But...I'm not a doctor."

"If he needs a doctor, just call me, and I'll get one. My number's preprogrammed." Mr. No-Name handed her a phone as Austin went on.

"And who should I ask for?" she asked, trying not to sound curious in the least.

Mr. No-Name let out a snort as if to say, *nice try*. "I'll know it's you."

Austin interrupted. "There's more oxygen tanks against the wall. Just keep him comfortable until we get back."

Andi looked between them. None of this made sense—not the cat, not this job, not this house, and definitely not these two extremely handsome, yet extremely odd men. "Where are you going anyhow?"

Mr. No-Name shook his head at her question. "Out. But we'll return by dawn, and I promise you'll be on the first bus back to the city. Okay?"

Mr. No-Name's gaze pressed her, as Austin loomed.

She inhaled—to tell them how insane all this was and back out—but then she reminded herself that the only thing that needed to make sense was the fact that one night here would equal a month of her normal paycheck. She glanced at the patient and did her best to ping out with her inherent nurse-radar, honed by months of taking too many shifts, taking in his color, and the numbers on the screen. He was the most normal thing here, hands down. "Yeah, okay," she said, deciding. She pulled out the phone she'd been given and waved it at Mr. No-Name. "I'll call if anything happens; otherwise, I'll see you in eight."

"Good," Mr. No-Name said and smiled at her—fully—for the first time all night. The sensation of his pleased attention on her was almost as bad as whatever had happened to her on the road here. She wanted to run away, but she found she couldn't. She was struck—pierced—like she was a deer in headlights. He was just too much.

Then the cat leapt off the bed and wound around Mr. No-Name's legs. He glanced down, and the moment was over. The spotlight had moved on. She sagged, caught herself, and hoped he hadn't seen it. It didn't seem like he had as he knelt down to knuckle the cat's head softly.

The cat meowed at him, repeatedly, as if it had strong opinions, and Mr. No-Name gave it a dour look. "No, she didn't bring anything for you," he told the cat, and then looked back to her. "If you hear any sounds in the house, just ignore them. It's an old house; it creaks a lot." Austin coughed from the door, and Mr. No-Name headed toward him. Her audience was over. The men left, and the cat followed them.

Andi relaxed, then became embarrassed by how she'd felt. What was she, some kind of schoolgirl? *You know better!* Whoever she'd been in the moment he'd looked at her—stupidly happy, foolishly hopeful, and just a teensy bit terrified—it wasn't the real her.

The real Andi was a nurse who knew what to do—every time, all of the time.

She went to the bed, unlooped her stethoscope from her neck, and started to assess her patient.

CHAPTER
TWO

"What'd Grim say?" Austin asked Damian on their way to the garage.

"That she's too small to be of any use." In reality, Grimalkin had asked if Andi had brought him any cheese, the bluer, the better—because the house was out. Luckily, Damian was the only one who could understand the hugely powerful multidimensional guardian he'd been assigned at birth, so no one else knew how easily a gift of cheese would distract him.

"For once, the cat and I agree. If my brother wakes up –"

"I know," Damian said, shutting down further conversation. If Zach woke up while they were gone—a big *if*—then hopefully he and the nurse could have an intelligent conversation, after which she'd take off his restraints. He'd be confused about what had happened, but he'd be smart enough to realize she was an outsider.

He got into the armored SUV, waiting with some of the rest of his crew. It was just him and the guys tonight. Max was driving, Jamison had his eyes on his electronics, and he sat close to Austin who was busy wiping down the barrel of something black and shiny.

He sank back into his seat, thinking about the nurse.

She smelled good, his dragon commented.

Shush, he told his dragon—but it was right.

Oil, plastics, but more overwhelmingly, the aroma of iron, surrounded him. Humans had so much iron in their blood; it was a wonder to him that they weren't magnetic. Living in human society, he had gotten used to the metallic scent, but for some reason, tonight it seemed more pungent than usual.

It was all because of her.

When she had gotten into the car, the gaseous stink of the bus she had been on and the medicinal chemical scents that were a hallmark of her occupation clung to her coat. Those were expected.

But underlying all that was her own subtle scent, undetectable to most humans, and yet abruptly mouthwatering all the same.

Apples and caramel, yes, that's what it reminded him of—and saltwater.

How strange.

He swiped through his emails, opening the unread files Mills had sent over. Top of her class in community college and then nursing school. But she'd suffered student loans, a staggeringly high amount of debt owed to a hospital which looked like medical bills for a relative before it got wiped—presumably by that relative's death—and a brother who apparently couldn't resist taking rides in cop cars. Which made her perfect for his purposes: hungry enough to be looking for cash, smart enough to keep Zach alive, and hopefully, smart enough to not ask many more questions. There was always the Forgetting Fire if she got too curious. He reached the end of her background check and found she lived in a gentrifying part of town in an apartment above a Greek bakery. That explained her scent. Her apartment probably smelled entirely of baked goods.

Mystery solved, Damian put the phone back into his pocket. But his mind went right back to her. *Andi.* What an odd name for a girl. He had the strangest urge to say it out loud, irrationally, to see if the sound tasted as good as she smelled. And that interesting streak of blue that he'd glimpsed a flash of before she'd wound her dark hair up—something about the act of her hiding it made him want to unwind and expose it again, to possibly feel the wrap of it around his hand.

"Why'd you warn her about the house?" Austin asked Damian, distracting him from his thoughts.

"Because Grimalkin doesn't like strangers."

"He doesn't like anyone," Austin countered.

"He's keeping an eye on Zach, isn't he?" Max said from the driver's seat, defending Damian's guardian's integrity. Damian knew his cat and his old weapons master got along—they had to; they were the only two things that'd come from the Realms with him, albeit at different times. The battle armor Max had on made the whiteness of his skin around it even more shocking, and Damian knew if he had his hat off, all his hair would be ghostly pale. He'd had an albino's pale eyes, too, before he'd lost them in a fight with another bear-shifter. Mills had replaced them with something magical hidden by goggles, turning him into the perfect bearer of Damian's Forgetting Fire, since its powers no longer seemed to work on him. And whatever kind of eyes he had now, he could snipe an Unearthly creature down at eight hundred yards.

"Grimalkin's probably hoping that he'll die," Austin said darkly.

Max broke into a toothy grin. "Nah, if Grimalkin wanted either of you dead, you'd be dead already, puppy."

Austin snorted at him. "Better to be a wolf who's a fighter than a bear who's a chimney sweep," Austin muttered, before addressing Damian again. "Was she sensitive enough for the perimeter to bother her?"

"Definitely."

Austin grunted. "How'd she do?"

"Admirably, considering she didn't know she was being magically attacked." There were several concentric security rings around his mansion, some magical, some not. He'd both seen and tasted her panic as they'd driven over one of them—the one Austin had been supposed to turn off. He'd seen other men throw themselves out of moving cars in fear and not know why to crawl crying back downhill. While she'd been scared, Andi hadn't run. Another interesting point.

"Do you think she bought it?" Austin asked, pretending to put a driver's hat on.

Damian knew he meant the subterfuge of him pretending to be a driver in his own employ. He'd wanted to meet the person taking care of Zach, to get a feel for her—he hadn't expected for him to wind up being so intrigued.

"Doesn't matter," he answered. "Either she doesn't figure it out, fine; or she does, and the fire will make her forget."

"Why bother? No one would believe her. She'd just be another internet crackpot," Jamison said while staring intently at the computer on his lap, as immersed in it as Austin was his weapons. He was very dark-skinned and lean in opposition to Max's bright whiteness and Austin's bulk, and between the hardware on his lap and the hardware of his arm that they'd replaced with tech, the man was practically half-computer.

"You mean, like you?" Austin said, goading the younger man.

"Don't make me change your Netflix password," Jamison snarked, then waved his hand for silence. "We're approaching the source of the signal. Slow down, Max."

Max grunted an acknowledgement. He was driving what Damian called "the tour bus." It was a heavily armored SUV, fortified with metal shielding, bulletproof glass, blast-resistant undercarriage, and, more importantly, personally warded by the most powerful witch on this side of the Pacific. Damian knew where they were by scent—the saltwater, gas, and oil fumes could only be from the familiar miasma of the docks—and they were here because somewhere nearby there was an Unearthly creature they needed to kill.

A few days ago, a gate had opened in Damian's domain. Gates were random rifts or tears between this world and other Realms, occurring when and where Earth and other Realms overlapped, allowing Unearthly things through for as long as the passage remained open. They could be as small as an atom, leaking a slow trickle of matter through that didn't belong—making exposed non-magical humans think they saw Bigfoot, UFOs, or ghosts—or they could burst open like lanced boils, letting creatures that Ought Not Be through, flying, crawling, or oozing out to wreak havoc on whomever was unlucky enough to encounter them. Damian and his crew's job was to kill the monsters, seal the gates, and wipe the minds of any human left alive.

They'd easily closed the most recent gate fifty miles outside of town, but not before three sizable creatures had made it through. The one they'd decided was the most dangerous, that needed to be put down instantly, had been an insectoid creature the size of a bus with bulletproof chitin and webbing that had been tougher to cut than steel cables. It'd been impervious to fire, too—at least human fire. Which was why Damian had had to let himself go.

They'd corralled the monster in a low canyon, but it'd slithered up a wall and over the defensive line Damian had created for the men, cutting him off from them. Zach abandoned his post, ran to help, and gotten grabbed. He'd screamed—and Damian could still hear those screams, agonized and terrified, now—and Damian had changed in an instant. From the human that he pretended to be, to the dragon that he *was*.

Massive. Mindless. Monstrous.

Angry.

His dragon ended the creature in moments, reveling in the freedom and destruction, flipping the thing over to claw through its underbelly. Afterward, Damian had struggled to regain control. It hadn't been easy.

"How much farther?" asked Max through gritted teeth.

Damian could feel the preparatory intensity of his crew as they waited quietly for Jamison's next instruction. Between Zach's injury and losing Michael last year…. Just because they were good at what they did didn't mean it was safe.

"Almost there. We've gotta pass it to triangulate it. Just keep going," Jamison said, oblivious to everything but the data he was harvesting on his screen.

Damian had told Jamison and Mills to prioritize creating technology to predict when gates were opening, so they could preemptively seal them before the Unearthly came through. They were gaining ground, but until they managed to perfect it, members of his team would always be in danger—and so would Damian. Because every time he shifted, his dragon came closer to claiming—and keeping—control.

"Stop," Jamison said, closing his metal hand into a fist.

The vehicle downshifted, and the men hurried to finish arming themselves as Damian thought of everything he'd given up to get this far, everything he'd put his men through—all the Unearthly they'd faced, losing Michael, and now, nearly losing Zach.

"Whoa," said Austin, looking at him askance, and Damian realized he was exhaling smoke. "Let's keep it together this time, 'kay?"

Damian narrowed his eyes at him. "Zach almost died."

"I know," said Austin with a dispassionate look on his face. "He's my brother. But that doesn't change things."

Damian held his gaze, fighting the urge to let his eyes flare with magic.

The very same thing that gave him purpose, which made him a member of this team, was also the very thing that put them all at risk.

His own Unearthly heritage.

Of all of them, Austin was the one who never forgot what Damian was. And when he finally turned, becoming draconic without hope of turning back, Damian knew without a doubt that Austin would be the one to put him down.

"Which one's here tonight?" Max twisted around to look back now that they were parked. "The lady or the tiger?" They'd all seen the other two creatures they'd passed over in favor of killing the bus-bug thing.

"Hang on." Jamison's magical equipment wasn't anywhere near

as sensitive as Damian was at this range. He closed his eyes and reached out with his senses. The all too familiar red magic bloomed in his mind, shaping itself into a vision of the source. He felt the fiery warmth that all creatures from the Unearthly side had—and more—longing, desire, and urges that made his heart beat faster and his heat sink low.

"The lady," said Damian

Everyone groaned. It wasn't that they couldn't take down a succubus. They were pretty frequent Unearthly escapees—it was just the aftereffects that made things difficult.

"It had to be a fucking succubus," said Max with a groan. "They're creepy as hell, once you get down to the real monster underneath."

"Agreed," Austin said, then turned to Damian. "What's this one look like?"

He concentrated on the spark again.

"In the other Realm, it has white wings, along with the tentacles," he said finally. "Here, it's got big breasts and blonde hair—a cross between a Christmas angel and a porn star."

Austin cursed, but reached for the net gun before stepping out.

They were indeed, as Damian had predicted, on the docks. Which was a strange place for a succubus to be working, unless there was some sort of pleasure cruise—an emphasis on pleasure—nearby. But Max had his goggles on, scanning nearby buildings. "Over there," he said and pointed. Once he had, Damian could feel it too, without any technological or magical enhancements.

Somewhere, in one of these buildings, was a bass-heavy beat.

An illegal warehouse party at the docks attracting a succubus? Sounded about right. "Spheres, Jamison?"

"Catch." The other man reached into a belt holster and retrieved marble-sized magical objects to toss to each of them. Damian caught his and felt a layer of magic envelope him as they walked down the alley. It wasn't there to protect him, so much as to protect other people from him—and the crew. No one wanted to see their group of overly muscled and beweaponed men walking down the street, so the sphere showed them whatever they wanted to see instead—men without guns, puppies, lost balloons. Damian didn't question the sphere's judgment, he just knew that they worked.

"The only thing is..." Austin began, as they got closer to the sound.

"We'll still need a victim to lure it away," Damian said, finishing his statement. He unholstered his gun to hand it over to Jamison.

"How come only you get to talk to the pretty ladies?" Jamison teased.

"Because I'm immune to their charms. And if this one is as bad as it feels, it has very nasty knives." He handed his sphere over, too, leaving the safety of its magic behind. The others were all in tactical gear, but he'd kept on the suit he'd worn to pick up Andi. He didn't need gear when there was a sixty-foot, fire-breathing reptile inside him longing to get out and fuck shit up.

Max cracked the knuckles on one hand. "Where do you want us?"

Damian scanned the building. Two huge men were bouncing in front of a door that was practically vibrating with the bass from the building behind it. The building itself only had small windows up at the top, strobing red and gold with the lights from inside, which meant external visibility was shit, but he had a feeling he'd be able to lure the thing out.

"Southeast exit's best," Jamison said, looking at schematics on a tablet. "The other buildings there form a natural cage."

"Done," Max said, jogging to the warehouse's far side. Jamison saluted Damian with his metallic arm and ran off in the other direction—which left him and Austin alone.

"Try not to have too much fun before the hurty bits," Austin said with a smirk, then went to head around back. Damian counted to twenty to give them all time, then headed toward the door with his most wicked smile.

. . .

Getting in was the easy part—a hundred-dollar bill did that—but he stood out once inside, very different from all the riotous dancers. He was GQ, and they were all sweaty, high, and half-dressed—a wild throng of humanity.

More like prey, grumbled the creature inside him.

He ignored it and made sure the southeast exit was feasible. It was at the end of a hallway and not blocked by pallets or locked with chains.

"Southeast is a go. Going silent now," he replied, taking out his earpiece before walking toward a makeshift bar created out of pallets and storage boxes. He didn't blame the succubus for coming here; he would've liked to've done so himself, as a human. To just be able to let everything go—and to know that everything would still be safe and okay.

He didn't have that liberty.

Damian closed his eyes, pulsing the powers inside him out to search for her like radar. Once, twice, three times and the beast would feel him, but it didn't matter, he had her—in the middle of the dance floor. A group of men and women circled her, thinking they were enjoying themselves. He knew if he let his gaze go draconic, he'd see her true form—wings tucked back as her waist-high tendrils spun out to spike everyone nearby. Everyone she speared would think they were in love—with her, with here, with life, it wouldn't matter—and if she wasn't stopped, she'd drain them of energy until they became her mindless slaves.

He ordered a shot of whiskey and downed it at the bar before heading to the dance floor. This wasn't the place to sip. If he was going to get her to follow him outside, he needed to seem fully human, and every human here was drinking. The group of people around her had grown from five to ten; he needed to act quickly, but he hesitated intentionally, like he was unsure, and made sure to catch her eye on a spin.

She had hair like the sun, and it swirled around her like her tendrils would have if he'd allowed himself to see them. He stood at the edge of the dance floor, looking rich and cruel and disapproving —not taking his eyes off of her—daring her to come to him.

She was like a cobra dancing with a snake charmer, doing everything in her power to lure him closer into tendril range. But that wouldn't do. He needed her alone, so he watched her studiously, letting her know he was interested, but not content to be amongst the commoners.

One by one, dancers seemed to come out of their reverie and stumble to the edges of the dance floor as she released them, not knowing how close they'd come to losing their lives. He had to fight not to smile. This wasn't his first time with a succubus; they were all alike—completely certain in their abilities to torment humans and completely unable to ignore a challenge.

She was close now, still dancing, but just for him. She was wearing next to nothing, the thigh-high slits of her skirt showing off her legs as she moved, as she kept moving hypnotically, coming closer. He could smell the addictively sexy pheromone she emitted and almost wished it worked on him because it was hard to stay still knowing that once she came a few steps closer she would strike.

She smiled winningly and the first tendril hit—straight through his heart. The dragon half of him bellowed and rose and fought, and he had to wall it off as quickly as he could. *Calm down. Now!*

He did his best impersonation of a struck human for her. "You," he whispered, his voice low.

"You-you're different." Her voice was a purr with an inhuman thrum underneath.

She struck another tendril through him, and instead of screaming, he had to pretend to be enamored. "I want you." In real life, he would never be that abrupt, but bewitched humans had no common sense.

"That's good," she purred. "I want you too." She reached her hand up and touched his face. "I'll tell you a secret. I want everyone here."

He smiled at her, pretending to be innocent, trying to ignore the way he could feel the spears of her magic slide in and out of him, sucking at his essence. Her hand trailed down his chest and seemed certain to go lower.

"Me first?" he offered.

Kill her! the dragon in him growled.

SHUT UP! he commanded.

"Oh, yes. You first," she agreed, letting her hand sink to his waistband. He reached for her and dragged her close, kissing her hard, before she could feel that he wasn't—that he was the only thing not turned on by her within thirty feet.

"I need you," he said, coming up for air like a desperate man. The things she was doing to his brain and inside of him—a migraine blossomed, and it was hard to stay clearheaded—and his dragon howled. "Outside?"

She smiled at him, and with his dragon this close, it looked like all her teeth were fangs. "Yes," she agreed, and together they stumbled toward the southeast exit.

DAMIAN WASN'T sure what shape his crew's attack would take, as he made out with the creature down the hallway toward the southeast door. He ignored the pain, trying to concentrate on the feel of its breasts against him and not letting it lock him in against a wall.

Then they reached the door, and he shoved her outside, blocking the door with his own body. He didn't want the succubus running back into the crowd as they shot her with warded guns. No one would get hurt, but the chaos they'd cause could create a stampede.

Every single thing they fought with was warded—right down to the bullets. Which meant they wouldn't hurt normal humans—just Unearthly things.

Like him.

Which also meant he was in harm's way.

"Move!" Austin shouted at him. The succubus took in her surroundings—the blinding phosphorescent lamps his crew had set up, the guns that were trained on her.

"Whaaat?" Her voice rose with an unholy pitch. "No—I did not escape the depths of—"

A sniped shot—Max, from a nearby building, Damian knew—came through her neck, blowing out her throat. He could almost hear the bear-shifter saying, "Don't care," as he silenced her. Damian threw her forward with all his might, felt the tendrils releasing for a second as they moved with her, and then they grabbed on harder. He sank to his knees as she drained his strength, and with wide eyes, he watched her heal.

Unearthly things were stronger than Earthly ones, yes, but they didn't heal like that. Maybe Max had only grazed her? But then why was his shirt streaked with so much blood?

His thoughts took only half a second, and then he heard Jamison call his name. "Damian! Catch!"

Jamison was throwing his weapon to him, and the succubus batted it down with a now-visible wing. It didn't matter, though. Austin was advancing—pumping rounds into her—and Max was still sniping her from afar, and slowly, the human shell of what she appeared to be was blasted away until only the monster of what she was shone underneath the phosphorescent lights. Their weapons pushed her back out of striking range and then Damian was free. She sank to her knees, her tendrils writhing desperately around her, searching for fresh victims.

"No," she whispered as she realized she was dying. An iridescent purple eye swung in an overlarge socket to spot him. "You and I...we are the same. I felt it in you. Why do you align yourself with them when you could have flown with me?"

Damian didn't have an answer for her; he just stood and picked up his gun. This needed to be over. He squeezed off a round into her head as the tendrils that had pierced him snaked weakly by his ankles.

"I will crawl into you and eat your soul," she threatened, from a mouth that spontaneously appeared on her neck as Jamison brought a lamp closer.

"Pity for you, I don't have one," Damian said and fired the shot that finally ended her.

CHAPTER THREE

It was very easy to creep yourself out at the hospital at night.

Everything in a hospital was industrialized. There was a veneer of warmth in patient spaces—warm lights, nice murals, wood paneling—but underneath that, in the guts of the hospital, things were usually poorly lit and dusty. Hallways full of empty beds with restraints still attached to them. Baby incubators with broken lamps. Pipes that knocked and wheels that creaked.

And that was before you got to any of the people dying.

Because she didn't know how many people had died in this house—it was so old, she was absolutely positive that multiple people had—Andi did what she always did to make herself feel better. She threw all the lights on.

They sputtered to life like the wiring was old, but they brightened the room a little—enough to keep her spirits up, for now.

And after that, it was time for nursing. A full assessment. Just like she was at work, that's all she had to pretend.

She walked over to the patient's bed. Normally she'd have started off by trying to wake him. Even though he was unconscious, he looked strong. That, and the uncompromising way with which

Austin'd restrained him—barely any slack on either wrist—made her second-guess herself. Instead, she just lifted up his eyelids to make sure his pupils moved.

After that, airway—he was breathing on his own, albeit with an oxygen mask—and circulation—all of his IVs were good, plus his rate on the monitor was normal. Last but not least, a quick head to toe. She lifted up the sheets. It wouldn't do to wait eight hours to find out he had a pool of blood growing underneath him, hidden by the linens.

She was surprised to find him naked underneath. He was ridiculously well-muscled. Half of his torso was covered by a large bandage, and what wasn't was covered in even more tattoos, just like his arms. They were old...formal...and strange. Like words written in a language she not only couldn't understand, but had never seen before, and she considered herself pretty damn worldly. Or at least she'd watched a lot of National Geographic.

They were almost like...hieroglyphs? But not quite.

Andi ignored the tattoos and went back to frowning at the dressing, mad at herself for not assessing her patient before Austin'd left. It went from his hip to his shoulder, and it was too big to be from surgery. How would they have performed surgery here? Surely, they weren't *that* old/rich/crazy. It had pink drainage on it. She put on gloves to touch it and found it saturated.

Which meant it wasn't doing him any good and needed to be changed.

Andi looked around the room. This wasn't civil war times; surely, she wasn't going to use a half-stuffed pillow. Austin had brought the crash cart in from somewhere. Maybe there was a medical supply room down the hall?

"Be good," she commanded her patient and trotted down the way she thought Austin had gone.

• • •

What Mr. No-Name hadn't mentioned about the house was that it was very nearly a labyrinth.

Though, now that she thought about it, Mr. No-Name-With-a-Fancy-Watch was probably a Blackwood himself. Maybe a distant cousin or something. She had once read a book about a rich family who hired lesser relatives to keep their secrets. Maybe that's how the Blackwoods rolled.

She went through rooms that didn't make sense—one filled with wrapping paper. Did Mr. Blackwood really send so many gifts?—a bedroom, a mudroom—even though it didn't connect outdoors—a kitchenette, a game room, a tiki bar, a closet with enough furs in it to lead to Narnia. She counted rights on her right hand and lefts on her left hand and was able to make it back, but she hadn't found anything useful. Not even a bathroom. Or a coffeepot.

When she returned, there was a sterile chest vest in its package, sitting on the patient.

The first thing Andi did was to check the patient's restraints. Because if this was his idea of a "fun game," then she was going to strangle him until he really needed that oxygen mask. But he was just like she'd left him; he hadn't moved. Who the hell had brought her that?

"Hello?" she asked, not sure what would be worse—if no one answered her or if someone did. "Is anyone else here?"

She thought she heard an echo of her own voice but wasn't sure.

"Okay," she announced, stepping closer to him. "If someone is taping this to punk me later, let me just say preemptively that you're an asshole."

She yanked back the sheet dramatically, hoping to trigger something. When nothing happened—same hot patient, same slow bleed—she pulled on fresh gloves.

The patient's chest was hairless, which was good because she was ripping an awful lot of tape off of him. Apparently, Austin had never heard of abdominal binders—or maybe this dude appreciated the free wax. She snorted to herself as the last of the tape came free, and the soggy dressing slid off, revealing the wound underneath.

There was no way a "fall" had done that to him—not unless the stairs here grew claws and teeth. The end of the chest tube was expertly taped to his rib cage, like a sleeping snake, but underneath it was jagged rakes of red. It looked like he'd been clawed, but she couldn't begin to guess what'd done it. She held out her own hand for comparison and couldn't have done that to him even if she were Wolverine and her fingers fully spread. And then there was a...bite mark? Coming down over one shoulder? No wonder his lung had popped.

She glanced back up at his face. Had his head gotten hit, too, in his fight with whatever the hell this had been? Or had he just freaked the fuck out and gone catatonic? Because if something big enough to do this decided to pretend she was a cat toy, that's what she would do.

She frowned at his wound for a thoughtful moment, then expertly wrapped him up, making sure to pull the sheet up to his neck, exactly how she'd found him.

"I don't know what you got into, but I hope it doesn't get into me."

Then she walked away from the bed and sat on one of the library's leather couches.

THE DOWNSIDE of not having her own phone meant not having her ebook app for reading. She scrounged a few of the old books left on the library's shelves. Management at the hospital never got that you had to do something to pass the time at night—that some nights you weren't getting paid to work, so much as getting paid to just stay up and be there in case there was work to be done. She opened *The Count of Monte Cristo* and started reading.

Hours passed. At work, she'd nap on break, but there were no real "breaks" here to speak of, plus she sure as hell wasn't sleeping. She checked on the patient regularly, tried to pretend medical supplies hadn't just appeared when she needed them, and that there was a way falling down stairs could do that to a man.

Halfway through her book, she had a thought.

What if...the patient here really was Mr. Blackwood and they were torturing him so they'd get his fortune?

She looked from her book to her patient. No, she was just getting ideas from her book. It was almost five a.m. That was when everybody started feeling loopy. Humans just weren't meant to be up this late.

But what if... Whatever other crazy idea she was going to have evaporated when she heard a child's voice.

"Help me," it pleaded.

Andi jumped up and whirled, feeling her heart race in the silence.

Had she heard that? She had to have. She'd been up late plenty, and she'd never hallucinated before. And yet, just as she was about to talk herself out of it, she heard the voice again.

"Please, help me," it begged her from farther away.

Mr. No-Name hadn't mentioned anyone else in the house.

But for a house this big, it would be normal to have more staff, right? The staff was beneath attention and mention. But maybe Blackwood senior or junior or third cousin once removed was into Bad Things, and this was the only chance whoever needed help would have to escape to safety?

"Oh my God, can you hear me?" the voice sobbed in a desperate panic. "Please be real. Please...and come find me!" the voice cried.

Andi took one look behind herself at the patient—safely sleeping just the way he had all night long—and then went racing after the voice.

She tore through the strange house, following the voice as sometimes it sounded far away—sometimes closer—always pleading. If whoever was calling her felt safe enough to ask for help, they must really be alone.

"I'm coming!" she shouted. She finally felt like she was on the trail. The voice became louder, the calls more frequent, summoning her to a bedroom outfitted like a dungeon. The walls were lined in green velvet wallpaper with ornate patterns burned out against it, and black leather furniture-like objects were arranged tastefully—almost like art—if Andi hadn't known what they were for.

She ran through it at top speed into the next room and found herself in a room almost exactly like the basement of her first home when she was growing up. Orange shag carpet, tan wood paneled walls, with a green felt regulation pool table sitting in the center of it. Same dingy light overhead, the same scent of cigarette smoke lingering in the air.

"Are you kidding me?" she whispered as she stopped in her tracks. The balls were racked and ready to play. All she was missing was Danny, her partner in crime. Pool was their father's favorite hobby. They played it with him incessantly any time he visited, hoping that someday they'd be good enough to make him stay. Whenever he left, she and Danny would play against each other for hours, practicing for the next time. They'd win his love someday, they knew it....

"Help me!" begged the voice. It sounded like it was just one room away now. She ran for the door like her chalk-dusted memories were chasing her—so quickly she couldn't stop herself and wound up falling.

Into a pond.

Andi bobbed up for air, gasping, surrounded by lily pads as wide as dinner plates and peals of laughter.

"Stop that!" she shouted, looking up to see who was laughing and finding only another high ceiling with a star-like chandelier. The laughter didn't stop.

Someone was having a very elaborate joke at her expense.

She felt herself turning beet red and swatted at the hip high water, then felt her ankles sink. Somehow, the bottom of this koi pond—inside the house—was mud. She panicked and kicked her shoes off, losing them to the murky depths in her rush to swim to the pond's side and clamber back out the way she'd come. She was totally sodden, and now she didn't have any shoes. "Fuck you," she told her unknown assailant. "And fuck this."

The laughter stopped. There was a rustling behind her, and a chill went up her spine—the cat appeared. Grimalkin walked over and meowed at her with cross-eyed disapproval, before sitting on his haunches to lick a paw judgmentally.

"Do you believe this?" she asked him, gesturing to herself and her surroundings. Grimalkin started purring loudly in response, which sounded a bit like laughing.

"Get it together, Andi." She pressed the heels of both hands to her eyes until she saw flashes and composed herself.

This night was cancelled. The second she got her money she was leaving this crazy place.

She stomped back the way she'd come, racing through the green-walled dungeon and found herself back in the room with the patient three doors later. Andi stood in the doorway and blinked at the impossibility of it all.

"No way!" But he was still alive, at least. She glanced over the numbers on his monitor—all within healthy ranges—then realized she could hear herself dripping on the hardwood floor. She scurried over to where the bed was, but she wasn't sure dripping on a rug was any better. She remembered one of the rooms she'd been in earlier and dared to find the coat closet again.

Hiding inside of it, she took all her wet clothes off and pulled on a fur—huge, black, and fluffy.

She didn't even care if she got the fur dirty. At this point, Mr. Blackwater, or whoever the hell was laughing, deserved it. She just wanted to go home.

CHAPTER
FOUR

Damian felt like he had been shot, electrocuted, and stabbed.

What had actually happened was worse.

They'd killed the succubus, but before that, she'd wounded him. And for some reason, he wasn't healing as fast as she had. That, plus her residual effects, had the dragon inside him howling to be released, furious at the cage once more. He felt his muscles enlarging, hardening in response. With gritted teeth, he mentally forced the beast back.

"Did anyone else get hit?" he asked, looking around. Everyone present shook their heads, and he knew Max was safe in his sniper's roost.

"Good. I need to go," he said, and turned, heading blindly away.

"Don't think you can shirk cleanup crew next time!" Austin yelled. Damian ignored him.

It was harder to find cars to hotwire in these days of Uber, but he found one, practically pulling the door off its hinges to get inside. He'd have Mills figure out who owned it and recompense them later.

All he knew was right now was he really fucking needed to get home where he could make the walls around his dragon real.

The car started, and he did a bootleg turn to race for the Briars—thinking fast—trying to keep his human side active and his dragon half down.

All of them had been touched by succubi before. It seemed like they were always waiting just outside of rifts, waiting to lure the unwary. Their perceived beauty, their attention, and that pheromone kept their victims in line, while the succubi fed on them, night and day until their followers became mindless fanatics who would do anything the succubi asked—from killing their own families to disemboweling themselves for a smile.

Typically, after an adrenaline-filled hunt and exposure to the pheromones, anyone who had come in contact with the creature would have the urge to fuck everything that moved for the next few days.

It hadn't turned out like that for him.

No.

Instead, it had wakened the doubts inside of him and given them a voice.

He had taken the lead because, in the past, he'd proven immune to a succubi's touch. But tonight's had been different. More powerful than other ones they had previously faced.

Come fly with me.

It was like the succubus had spoken directly to him. No, not to him, but to the dragon inside—the dragon who never got to fly when he wanted to, the dragon he kept with him on the ground.

Come fly with me.

He parked the car and stumbled out, ignoring the voice inside his head, pressing his hand to the keypad. The door unlocked, and he limped into the white marbled foyer.

Why the fuck had he decided to place his bedroom up all those goddamned stairs?

You could just fly.

Step by step, he dragged himself up the stairs, down the carpeted halls, and into his room, where he studiously avoided looking at himself in any of the many mirrors he used to communicate with other Realms. Right now, he was afraid of what he'd see. He didn't want to watch the dragon surging underneath his skin.

He opened the bottle of whiskey on his bar and chugged it until it was empty. It slid down his throat—a comforting warmth compared to the violence of the dragon fire within him. No one could get hurt, and all it did was make him sleepy. Grimalkin ran in and sniffed the air, likely catching a huge whiff of succubus pheromone. His hackles raised in an instant, his tail poofed, and he hopped back three feet with a wrinkled nose.

"I haven't smelled anything that bad since you brought me a stinking bishop." The cat shuddered and wiped its paw at its nose furiously. "Are you okay? And did you bring me any cheese?"

"Nice to see you, too, Grim." Damian flopped onto his bed, holding the empty decanter. Grimalkin jumped up onto the bed with him and leaned over, almost touching him nose to nose, slightly crossed blue-eyes full of concern.

"There's green blood on the ground. Is it yours?"

Damian shrugged. "I got hit a few times. Nothing I can't heal."

Grimalkin's tail lashed several times before he asked, "Did you return with as many as you left with?"

"Yes." Damian knew Grimalkin wasn't fond of everyone in his crew, but the cat was aware of how losing more men would hurt Damian.

"Good." Grim's nose was still crinkled, and his tongue was out, and Damian had the bizarre urge to tap it. Before he could do so, Grimalkin's eyes widened, pupils as dark as the night sky, as he segued into beg mode. "You know," Grimalkin said, voice low, like he was dying, "if you're gonna stink that bad, the least you could do is bring me cheese."

Damian tried not to laugh and failed. "Can't you just magic some up?" he asked for the millionth time.

"It's not the same." Grimalkin rubbed his head against Damian's jaw, muttering, "Just a little Port-Salut. That's all I'm asking."

"Oh my God, Grim," Damian said, pushing him away. "Okay, okay; I'll order some."

The cat perked up again, life returned. "No magic? Real cheese? Delivery drivers? To the front door?"

"Yes, I swear. But...tomorrow. It's late."

"So?" Grimalkin protested, teleporting Damian's phone onto the bed with them and into his hand. "Use the metal thing!"

"I'm not making someone deliver cheese here, Grim. It's almost dawn."

"But it's cheeeeeeeese," Grimalkin whined, looking forlornly at the phone in Damian's hand.

"I know," Damian said, dropping the phone to knuckle the cat's head. "But I'm not an asshole, okay? And if you'd rationed yourself better—"

"Rations? What's next, American slices?" Grimalkin said, and the house around them trembled, cat and domicile both quaking at the thought. "Do I look like I can survive on Jamison's Velveeta?" he asked Damian in all seriousness.

"No, of course not," Damian reassured the beast. "I'll do it tomorrow, I swear. Just...for tonight...I'm gonna need more of this. Please." He held up the decanter.

Grimalkin waved his tail petulantly, but then blinked his eyes slowly and obliged him, filling it with whiskey again. There were benefits to having a magical guardian assigned to you at birth—once you got past its odd dairy addiction.

Damian sat up, took another swig, and then dropped back down. "How's the girl?" Austin would have to take her home. He was in no condition—between the magical wounds he'd taken luring the succubus out, and the residual pheromones that Grim was scenting on him.

"Wet...and cheeseless," Grimalkin said, before staring at the spot where the wall met the ceiling and rubbing a paw behind one ear.

Damian had no idea what Grim meant by that, but he'd learned that sometimes it was better not to ask.

"Okay, then. Alone time. Now." He swept his arm sideways, making the cat jump neatly over his hand.

Grimalkin pounced on his fingers and bit them gently, mumbling around them. "But tomorrow?"

"Tomorrow. I swear."

The cat sprang off the bed and walked for the door. "Don't forget!"

"Like you'd let me," Damian said and ignored the pointed tail flick Grimalkin made in his direction. Despite how irritating his obsession could be at times, Grimalkin was the one thing from home he'd gotten to take with him from the Realms, and Damian was glad to have him.

Finally alone, Damian sat up. He was sore—sitting up made his head spin. He walked across his room to put the decanter back on the bar and took off his shirt.

You could've flown tonight. His own dragon now, emerging as he headed back to his bed, tormenting him with the succubi's words.

If it wasn't one beast bothering him, it was another. But where Grimalkin was concerned for him—at least, even if his own well-being came a close second to cheese for the cat—his dragon hadn't cared. At all. His dragon had watched the succubus torturing people on the dance floor and been totally unmoved. It didn't judge the succubus for doing what she needed to to survive, didn't find her violence disgusting or cruel.

What did it say about him that something so monstrous was a part of him?

It says I shouldn't have put the whiskey down so far away. Damian didn't get up to get it, though, instead choosing to close his eyes and will himself to sleep.

CHAPTER
FIVE

Andi's clothes were not dry by dawn. She was tired and wet and cranky, and the phone Mr. No-Name had given her said it was six a.m. Someone should be coming to relieve her soon, right?

Then she heard it—the sound of a door slamming from afar.

Was it real? After her experiences earlier tonight, she doubted it. Then she heard another door, somewhere deeper in the house.

If whatever lived in this house wanted to torment her, pretending to be distantly slamming doors was an odd way to do it, which made her think that the sounds were real and that someone had gotten home a little early.

Good, then that person could take her the fuck away from here—after paying her handsomely, of course. Nothing about her patient had changed overnight. She'd done a good job, in spite of everything else.

She put her wet clothes in the bag the dressing supplies had come in so they wouldn't drip and then decided to hunt down the person who'd slammed the doors.

Andi walked back to the entryway—the path seemed about two

rooms shorter, but she wasn't going to question that right now—and found herself in front of the main door, with the staircases behind her. She turned, and the spiral one up to the ceiling that'd caught her eye earlier was gone now.

Of course, it was.

She swallowed and fought the urge to rub her eyes again.

"Hello? I need to go home now."

No one answered, not even to laugh. She stood equidistant between the two stairs—they both led to opposite wings of the house. She could waste hours looking for someone here. A splash of emerald green caught her eye—on the stairs to her right. It wasn't pondwater from her escapade earlier. She'd never made it up to the front of the house; she was sure of it. No, it looked like someone had spilled...cough syrup. And there was a trail of it—heading up.

She was only seventy percent sure she hadn't seen the trail coming in, but it was enough. She held the fur coat tighter around her waist and followed it up the stairs.

The green stains led her down endless halls, doors that were bolted from the outside, and past judgmental looking statues until they reached a door. Perhaps the second one she'd heard shut earlier? She leaned against the outside of it, and would've sworn she heard someone stirring inside. She rapped on it gently. "Hello?"

No one answered. But it, unlike the other doors she'd passed by, wasn't locked. She twisted the handle and opened it up.

The room inside was huge—palatial even; it could've bunked an army. One wall was lined with books—the older, the better, it seemed—with chairs and a bar, and then another wall was just mirrors, which was a little creepy. They were all different shapes, with separate ornate frames, and all their glass was fogged. Who the hell collected this many mirrors, and why? *Rich people—with bad taste.*

And then, in the middle of the room, near the windows which were letting in light from the oncoming dawn was Mr. No-Name, lying shirtless in the middle of a very large bed. The green stains clearly led up the carpeting directly to him.

*No, no, no...*enough weirdness for the night. This was not something she would be investigating. *Hellllll, no!*

But Mr. No-Name's features were softer now that he was asleep. And he looked...just like the pictures of Damian Blackwood that she'd googled up—the old, grainy ones that were scanned in from old newspapers with no originals. And...also a lot like the younger one with the same name she'd read about too—the asshole cousin with the fancy car and a different girl on his arm every weekend.

None of that explained why he was bleeding green, though.

There are dragons in this world, my dear. Real dragons.

She crept up to the bed's edge. If only she knew how to drive, then she could just rifle through his clothes for car keys.

"Hello?" she asked again at the foot of the bed, tempted to knee the mattress. "Hey...I want to go home now."

When he didn't stir, she leaned in and caught a whiff of something that was the worst stink she'd ever smelled—no small feat considering she was an ICU nurse. Her nose wrinkled, her body recoiled, and then...bliss. Like a good night with girlfriends after drinking a whole bottle of wine, or like the haze you got before an Ambien made you go to sleep. Soft and gentle bliss. She was safe, and she knew she wouldn't have to worry about anything ever again. Things...everything—her job, this job, her missing brother—finally felt easy.

And Mr. Blackwood—who'd already been the hottest man she'd ever seen in person—was now utterly irresistible.

Sure, he was bleeding electric green fluids from a gash between his ribs, and she should definitely be concerned about that—said a small and shrinking part of her mind—but why not just take a moment to appreciate the perfection of the rest of him, first? Andi put a knee on the mattress and slowly crawled up on the side opposite the bleeding to get a better look. She hadn't seen him with his shirt off yet, after all. She hadn't known the way his strong hands became muscular arms, the kind that could pick a girl up and carry her off without even trying. The way his shoulders framed his torso, and the way the muscles made his chest worth licking, down to a ripple of abs and a fine trail of hair leading down...

She was practically hovering over him now and while—*this is out of character for you! Stop it!*—howled inside from somewhere far away, the rest of her wanted to know everything about him. How he smelled, how he tasted, how it would feel when she touched him, and how it would feel when he touched her...preferably deep inside.

Would he mind?

She brought her hand up to brush the angular slope of his cheek.

"Hey," she whispered.

His golden eyes fluttered open, taking her in, and they had an oddly inhuman sheen. "Hmmm?"

"Wake up," she urged him. "Wake up enough to say yes."

He blinked. "Yes to—"

She leaned forward and planted her lips on his, swallowing whatever he was going to say next. In an instant, his head tilted to make his mouth fit hers perfectly, letting her tongue push in, and his hands were rising up the inside of the fur coat she'd stolen downstairs. Then he was fiercely kissing her back, his lips urgent against hers, his tongue pressing into her mouth, and although she was the one hovering above him, it felt like she was falling in—into what, she didn't know—but she never wanted to land. This was what she'd always been looking for, and she hadn't even known it.

One of his arms circled her waist, pulling her closer to him, and his other hand slid up her ribs to hold her breast and swipe a thumb against her nipple as she melted into him. If need could be made manifest, she felt it pulse from him, and everything in her wanted to answer its call. She shivered and let go, her body asking him for more, ready for anything, when he rose up and pushed her back, roughly.

"What?" Andi wasn't sure precisely what she'd done wrong when all she wanted to do was make him happy.

"Goddammit," he said, his voice hoarse, looking at her, clutching his hand to his bleeding side. "Grim, please exchange all the air in this room now and don't stop till I say so."

"But I can explain!" she went on, even though she couldn't, as a sudden breeze sprang up from nowhere.

"No...just...be quiet." He put a hand out to stop her from talking, and she bit her lips to obey. He was so handsome and magical and smart! How had she ever thought she could ever leave his side?

"Listen, this isn't you." He rocked himself over to the side of the bed to stand, and Andi noticed the pool of green he left behind him had gotten larger in the meantime. "Just go outside, find Austin, and tell him to pay you and take you home. I need to go bathe."

Andi was torn between staying quiet like she'd been told and mentioning the blood, like the nurse-voice inside of her demanded. Her fear of him being hurt quickly won out over her fear of disobedience. "But, are you okay?"

"No," he growled without looking back at her. "You don't actually want me, and I have a completely inappropriate hard-on. I am not okay."

"Because of the green blood?" she guessed, trying harder to help him.

"What're you..." he said, turning back, seeing the trail of green he'd left behind, looking down at his own hand covered in the stuff. "Shit. Sometimes the scales make it hard to feel things." She didn't know what to make of that, or what he said next. "Why aren't I healing?" He reached for the wound and then gasped, before crumpling to the ground.

Andi watched in horror—was he dying? She'd only just found him!—and ran over to his side.

His blood was definitely green and seeping out of a large gash between his ribs. Fresh air was buffeting against her face now and kneeling on the ground beside him she could feel all her uncertainty return, closely followed by a steamroller of anxiety and a semi-truck of self-doubt.

What-what the hell had just happened? She'd almost jumped him—what the fuck? She knew she needed to get laid, but come on, *have some self-respect, girl!*

But nurse-mode came and saved her from a spiral of embarrassment and shame. Even if his blood was green—presumably, it needed a heart to pump. She felt for a pulse and watched for chest rise. He was alive, but something was hurting him—she could tell by the excruciated look on his face. She tugged his arm away from his chest to see better, positioning him until she could see the wound—where there was a thorn jutting out.

Or more like a stinger. Of a giant dead bee. And it was still pumping something bad into him.

What the ever-loving fuck? She desperately glanced around. There was a bar set on the bar with tongs for ice. She raced for them and returned.

"I'm pretty sure this is going to hurt," she warned him, then grabbed the stinger and yanked it out. Poison still dripped from its tip, and suddenly the bar tongs were a lot shorter than she wanted. She threw the thing across the room—tongs and all—and looked back at him.

"Mr. Blackwood?" She shook him gently. He was still breathing evenly. She didn't think he'd popped a lung—only the tear in his side kept leaking green blood. "Damian?" she prodded, taking a guess that seemed more possibly correct all the time.

He suddenly shook his head, and when he opened his eyes, they were as human as ever. He blinked at her, pushing himself up on his arms. "What're you still doing here? I thought you were a dream. And...what happened to your own clothes?" His hand reached for his side while staring at her. "Is that...one of my grandmother's furs?"

Andi clutched the coat defensively, suddenly aware she was wearing something that probably cost more than her monthly rent and not much else. "No. I mean...it may be...but I got lost, and I stumbled and fell into your pool."

He looked adorably confused. "My...pool?"

"No." She held up her hand and frowned at him. "You're leaking green; you don't get to ask questions. What the hell happened to you...*Damian*?"

He frowned at the use of his name, clearly surprised that she had figured it out. *Score one for me,* she thought.

"Did you get attacked by...whatever it was that attacked your friend?"

"Not today." He glowered at her. "You've completed your duties by staying the night. Now go away." He rolled up and onto his knees, to stand and walk away from her.

"You're kidding me, right?" she asked, following him. "You dripped a trail of blood all the way to your room." She pointed down at the ground, only the green stains were gone. They couldn't have been all in her head. She'd *seen* them. "Don't you want a report on your friend, whoever he is?"

"Is he alive?"

"Yes."

"Then it's fine. I'm fine."

"Like I haven't heard that before." She put her hands on her hips where they wouldn't be tempted to touch him. "Look, even though somehow you turn me into a walking sexual harassment case, I'm not going to leave you when you're bleeding. Even if it is green."

"I'll heal—"

"It was a huge gash! You're lucky I didn't call nine-one-one!"

Damian, now that she was sure it was him, took in a breath and released it, then held his arms up so she could inspect him. She walked a quick circle around him—he had abs like *fucking whoa*—and couldn't see the wound anymore.

She bit her lips and scanned the room. He was healed somehow, and there was no longer a pool of green blood on his bed, and she couldn't see where she'd thrown the stinger or the bar tongs, despite the fact that there was no one else in the room to move them.

"Satisfied?" he asked her.

"Not even vaguely," she said. She watched her phrase spark a challenge in his eyes, one he just as quickly quenched—his face losing all the softness it'd held when he'd been asleep or injured—returning to its cold and slightly disapproving baseline.

"Go find Austin. He'll pay you and take you home. Forget all the rest," he said. She didn't move a muscle, and he sighed. "Please, for the first time in your life—I'm sure—just do as you're told."

Her resolve to get to the bottom of things wavered. She'd already known this place was impossibly strange, but somehow, he was the strangest thing of all. Even without the insta-lust and green blood. There was just something...improbable...about him.

"Fine," she said with a sigh. She'd spent enough nights trying to convince doctors that things were going bad before lab values proved her right to know that no one wanted to listen to the unbelievable until they had to.

"Thank you," he said with a slight nod of his head. He turned and started walking toward what was presumably a bathroom. "Grab clothes from my closet and leave the fur behind. It has sentimental value."

Before she could respond, the door closed behind him.

CHAPTER SIX

When Damian closed the bathroom door, Grimalkin was waiting for him, sitting primly on the marble counter, tail lashing up and down.

"I put the stinger in your office for you and cleaned up all the blood."

"And not a moment too soon," Damian said, leaning back against the closed door. He wondered how long it'd take Andi to vacate the premises. She was right behind the door now, probably not even dressed, putting his clothing over her taut, tight body—that he'd gotten to briefly touch.

Why did you stop her? his dragon asked. Part of being a shifter was experiencing one another's feelings when paying attention, and when Andi had started kissing him, his dragon had been fully present.

Because it wasn't real. We stank of succubus.

His dragon pondered this. *It felt real to me.*

It had, hadn't it? It'd seemed like the most real of dreams. Waking up to a beautiful girl taking an interest in him, wanting him to take interest back. Everything in him had longed to answer her, and he would have done so, eagerly—thoroughly—if he hadn't remembered the succubus's scent.

You should have let her continue, his dragon said.

And not for the first time, Damian realized his dragon wasn't big on consent. It wasn't worth getting into with the beast. Especially because his dragon was inside him; it knew how hard he'd been tempted. He thumped his head against the door's solid wood. And if he kept thinking about it, he'd be as hard as the door behind him. Fucking pheromones.

"...and you told me that you would heal," Grimalkin said, pointing his tail at Damian for emphasis, and Damian realized he'd lost some of his cat's words while thinking about Andi. He pushed away from the door and into the here and now.

"I would have. Except for the succubus stinger in the way."

"That you didn't know that you were hit with."

"I'll admit I didn't check that closely."

Grimalkin wove his head back and forth in grand disappointment. "This is why you need a mate. It is easier to clean all the places that need cleaning if you have someone else's tongue helping you."

It wasn't the first time his protector had urged him to find someone—and, unfortunately, Damian knew it would not be the last. "I'm alive, Grim. I mean, come on, a stinger might've made me pass out with poison for a little while, but it's not like it would kill me."

Grimalkin jumped down to the bathroom floor and reached up with both front paws, planting one on each of Damian's thighs, gently pricking through his slacks with his claws. "If something happens to you," he began, and Damian leaned down to pay attention as his cat's eyes went so wide, they were almost all pupil. "Who is going to buy me cheese?"

Damian laughed and gently kneed the cat down. "It is tomorrow, now, isn't it?" he said, reaching for his belt buckle.

"Very much so. But you can shower first," Grimalkin allowed him, with a wrinkle of his nose.

THE SECOND DAMIAN WAS GONE, Andi tried a door that was not the bathroom, found his closet, and resisted the urge to just hide inside.

What on earth had just happened to her? She'd told Damian she wouldn't ask questions—of him!—but that didn't mean that she wouldn't spend the next three months asking them of herself. *What the hell?* Green blood? And the entirely inappropriate way that she'd pounced on him? That wasn't like her at all.

There are dragons in this world, my dear. Real dragons. Beware.

Auntie Kim's warnings echoed in her mind, and after the night she'd just had, dragons seemed downright sensible, so, sure, why not?

She tamped down her upcoming freak-out and found jeans that were far too long for her, cuffing them up and belting them tight, before rifling through his closet for a shirt. They were all dress shirts, so she picked the nearest one and tied it at her waist—if she'd tucked it in, it'd have gone down to her knees.

Last but not least, she put on the shoes he'd evidently kicked off on his way in—which were far, far too big on her, like clown shoes almost—and tried to remind herself that it didn't matter that she wasn't getting her own shoes back, because with what she was getting paid she could definitely buy new ones.

She caught a blurry glance of herself in one of the many bedroom mirrors on her way out. She looked like she was very ineptly playing dress up. Whatever! She just needed to take a shower at her own place—and crawl into her own bed and forget this unbelievably strange night—and forget him. She glanced back at the closed bathroom door and heard the water turn on. Whatever was going on here, he was at the center of it. He was trouble, for sure.

Incredibly hot trouble.

Andi growled at herself, then picked up her bag of wet clothes left by the bathroom door and stepped out of the room.

"HEY!" she yelled, her voice echoing through the apparently empty corridors. "Is anyone here?"

To her surprise, Austin was waiting for her by the time she got to the lower level, and he seemed surprised to see her. "Damian didn't take you home?"

"Nope," she said, as his eyes took her outfit in.

"Damian...took you to bed?" Austin guessed.

Andi rolled her eyes. Not for lack of trying on her part for a bit there. "Also, no, although not that it'd be any of your business if he had." She wondered what it meant that that'd been Austin's first guess—did Damian have a revolving door? He was rich and impossibly handsome; of course, he got laid—all the time, probably.

And none of those women had realized he wasn't human like she had.

"I pulled a weird purple thorn from him. He was bleeding green blood," she said calmly, watching Austin's reaction.

Austin looked at her, a mixture of surprise and wariness in his eyes, clearly wondering how much she knew, how much she would ask him to explain.

"Don't worry. He's fine. He told me to find you and have you pay me and take me home." She stopped, and Austin looked at her, clearly waiting for her to ask more questions—*questions she desperately wanted to know the answer to!*—but shit with her brother had taught her that sometimes it was better not to get involved. "Look, I'm tired and I'd just like my money and a ride to the bus stop."

Austin hesitated for long enough that she started to get worried, then shook himself and said, "All right. Wait here."

He returned with her coat and a large envelope. Before he handed it over, though, he glanced down. "Do you know those are eight hundred-dollar shoes?"

Andi stopped herself from gasping in time. "So?" she said instead, defiantly.

"And they're...men's shoes."

"I know. I can mail them back, all right?" She pulled her coat on roughly and found her own phone in its pocket. "I don't want to talk about what happened to mine. Just take me to the bus already."

He looked her up and down again. Something about her current situation made him uneasy—but it didn't stop him from leading her outside.

"Wait here."

She did as she was told, waiting on the mansion's marble stairs as Austin went to retrieve a car. Dawn was rising over the horizon, and from this height, the light spilled over the hills, making the morning breathtaking. A light breeze pushed the scent of roses her way and picked up a lock of her hair to play with.

Out here, it was like last night had never happened—like it wasn't even real. Like the entire night had been a bad dream—except for the part that hadn't been.

Him.

And her kissing him.

Whatever *he* was.

She was almost glad she hadn't asked questions because if Austin had lied to her—which, of course, he would've; he'd have to—she'd have started to doubt her own two eyes.

Because that blood had not been human. Maybe that green stuff was what they pumped you with when you were rich enough to get something to somehow live forever? She fought not to nervously laugh at herself. She'd be on the bus soon, and she didn't want to seem crazy with a fist-sized wad of cash inside her pocket.

But where was Austin? Was he ghosting her?

Maybe Damian was…a ghost? And that green stuff had been ectoplasm?

Andi put a hand to her head, feeling the edge of a no-sleep headache approaching, knowing she needed to get to bed soon before she could think about anything else stupid—crazy, impossible—and real.

And then, just like it'd been designed to set off a migraine, a klaxon started wailing from somewhere behind her.

Andi whirled to look back at the house. "What the—" she got out before the lights on the inside of the house went red, and the metal shutters started loudly rolling down outside, cutting through ivy and beginning to cover all the castle's windows.

"Fuck," she breathed as a car pulled up behind her.

"More like, oh, shit!" Austin said, getting out.

"What's happening?"

"No time to explain," he said, and just as she'd imagined earlier in the night, he picked her up and put her over one shoulder.

CHAPTER SEVEN

Andi was swung over Austin's shoulder and started hitting his back with closed fists. "Hey! What the fuck!"

Austin ignored her and started to run toward the garage. He swiped a keypad with his hand—she watched him do it through his armpit, and then ran with her inside, knocking the air out of her lungs with his broad shoulder. "Get your hands off of me!" She grabbed hold of his belt and used it to brace herself, trying to slide forward. He completely ignored these efforts and any impropriety, hitching her back up by her crotch.

"HEY!" she shouted, twisting to try to knee him in the head.

"It's for your own safety," he explained, grabbing hold of her waist again. She thought he was about to set her down, but no, he held her under his arm. Her hair swirled, blocking her vision, but then she heard a latch open, and he threw her into a tiny space with shelves and a metal plated floor.

Andi got to her knees and inhaled because she was an excellent curser in two languages and she was about to tell Austin off, but the look of fear on his face stopped her cold.

"Keep quiet. You'll be safe in here," Austin said and shut the door.

She heard it lock, heard him leave, and knew she was alone in the dark.

ANDI FELT around the edges of the space she was in. Judging by the curve of the ceiling and the way she was barely able to stand up all the way inside, she thought she was in a van.

"Fucking asshole serial killer," she muttered to herself. Sammy's fears were right.

She patted her pockets. Her phone must've fallen out of her pocket on the way here—same for her envelope of money. All this trouble, all for nothing, and now... She moved her way up to sit on what seemed like a bench.

"What the hell have I gotten myself into?" She brought her knees up to hug to her chest. Why the klaxon and why the shutters? It'd have been an elaborate ruse if all that had happened just to kidnap her now after she'd been here all night. Same thing for if they didn't want to pay her—a month of pay was a lot to her, but not to Damian and his eight-hundred-dollar shoes.

She pulled one of them off and beat it against the side of the van.

"Can anyone hear me?" she shouted, then thumped some more. "I'm in here! Let me loose!" She took out all her frustrations on the van's interior, beating on it like it was a piñata. "Get me the fuck out of here!"

When she was done, she threw herself back on the bench, exhausted and panting, just this side of crying herself to sleep when something thumped back hard enough to make the entire van rock.

"Hello?" she whispered. Why hadn't she thought about the freaking fist-sized bee stinger before she'd made that much noise?

The van rocked again, as whatever was outside hit it from the other side. Andi bit her lips not to scream and scurried underneath the bench, pressing herself against the wheel well, feeling the pattern on the cold metal floor press against her skin.

She breathed in and out into her coat—half to calm herself, and half to mask her breathing. Whatever was outside... *Oh, God...oh, God...oh, God.*

But it was gone now. Right?

Andi lay stock still trying to see in the dark, and phantoms came—the kind you get when you rub your eyes too hard. Shimmers of gold with stripes of green—only her eyes weren't closed. She was filled with a sense of unholy dread as she realized something was materializing inside the van with her.

In the coin toss between dying lying on the ground and dying trying to escape, escape won. She rolled herself out and up and ran for what she thought was the front of the van and searching against the wall there for something—anything to help her—and on her second panicked pass through, she found it—a latch so flat it couldn't catch on anything. She popped it open so hard she broke a fingernail, but then fluorescent light flooded through. The van was still in the garage. She crawled through the hole—no way it'd been meant for that, probably just a pass through, she was just lucky she was small—and fell into the van's cab.

The van rocked behind her, and she heard the sound of something slithering. She kicked the pass-through shut and lunged to lock it just in time. A solid thump jarred her.

Whatever was back there was pissed. She whirled in the driver's seat, looking for something to protect herself with, and caught the glint of keys. In the ignition. Because when you had your own garage inside your own fortress, there was never any reason to take them out. She froze for an instant, trying to remember how it was that people did these things in movies, then twisted the keys wildly. The engine sputtered, and lights came on. She stomped at pedals indiscriminately, and the van threw itself backward. She heard it hit god knew what, but more importantly, whatever was inside the van had fallen backward—hard.

Her panicked hands scrambled over the console, trying to figure out what was what and put the van into D because it had to be for Drive, didn't it—if R was for reverse? And then she stomped on one pedal. Nothing happened, so she stomped on the other, and the van lurched forward, racing fast.

"Oh, shit!" she shouted, as the entire van ran into the garage door and it rocked forward. She kept her foot on the gas and heard the tires spinning as they tried to crawl up the bent doors.

"Come on!" She shoved herself forward as if her own slight weight would somehow help things as a shimmering began beside her. "Oh...no...come on!" She beat her hands on the steering wheel, and the van revved up a fraction of an inch higher—high enough for the wheels to catch on some mechanism of the door itself, pull itself almost vertical, and then the weight of the van crushed the garage door down and forward like a soda can. The van ran over the remains of the door, bouncing like it was going over craters on the moon, and then headed straight toward the fountain she'd thought was so pretty in the night. She only had time to scream before she crashed into it.

She was flung forward, and the steering wheel knocked the breath out of her. Gasping, she rolled toward the door, her foot still on the gas. The thing shimmering beside her hadn't stopped. It was growing more solid, and she didn't want to know what it was. The mere fact that it still existed in daylight meant that it was bad. The klaxons hadn't stopped alarming; they were louder now that she was outdoors. Andi opened the door and fell—the van had jumped onto the fountain's wall, leaving a three-foot gap between her and the ground. She landed on her forearm and scraped the shit out of it, shouted in pain, and then crawled away until she could gather herself enough to run—only to find that there was a golden-metallic shimmering ahead of her now.

She crouched, panting. She'd lost one of Damian's shoes, her elbow was bleeding onto his dress shirt, and there was a thing hunting her—was it real? It had to be. She took off Damian's other shoe and threw it at the golden glow, only for it to bounce back.

That seemed like an inherently bad sign. "Oh, no."

More and more of the striped monster—that was the only word

she had for it, that had to be what it was—was forming. Too many limbs and three tails; it was like a cross between a tiger and a centipede, and it had an almost human face that wouldn't stop grinning.

Andi drew in on herself. The thing could move through walls. There was nowhere she could go that it wouldn't be able to touch her. She was going to die here, and she wouldn't know what killed her.

CHAPTER
EIGHT

Damian heard the klaxons halfway through his shower and was tempted to blow them off. Trust Austin to run a drill after the longest night they'd had in a while.

But if they weren't a drill, it meant a perimeter breach. What on earth—or off it—could penetrate their barriers?

The shimmer-tiger. Damian hit the shower off and stalked into his bedroom without thinking. Shimmer-tigers were nasty affairs. They weren't fast, but they were sneaky, and their ability to teleport—albeit slowly—gave them an advantage over what other Unearthly creatures lacked.

It would be foolhardy for a shimmer-tiger to come after him directly. But he had plenty of humans and semi-humans in his employ, plus—he heard the sound of a violent crash and a distant, high-pitched scream.

"Open this window, now," he commanded, and Grimalkin obeyed, whipping the shutter up. He could see the roundabout, three stories down, where a steaming van had crushed his fountain, and Andi was curled up, surrounded by the materializing tiger on three sides. For once, both he and his dragon agreed—he punched the window's glass out, throwing himself through it as a man, knowing he would land as his dragon.

IN HER TIME AS A NURSE, Andi had watched a lot of patients die, and she'd learned there were three types of death:

The easy, quiet kind that struck in the night, and you knew no better before you went.

The kind that came up and walloped you—massive heart attack, massive pulmonary embolism, burst aortic aneurysm—that killed you so fast you hardly had time to be afraid.

But to her mind, the worst was the in-between kind. The strangle-some kind. Where you were aware of what was happening—when you couldn't get enough air, or when the chemo stopped working—and there was absolutely nothing you nor science could do about it.

And that's what it felt like was happening now.

That…that…that…*thing* was coming after her, and it didn't matter what she did or where she went, it wasn't going to stop, and she knew with every fiber of her being that whenever it did catch up with her, it wasn't going to just kill her. No, she could tell by the insane grin on its face that it was going to hurt…

Glass broke from somewhere far above, and it felt like it was the sound of her sanity giving way. It rained down, and she heard it land on stone and water, and then something cast a shadow over her like a low-flying plane. She threw her arm up to protect herself and then gasped as a dragon landed.

If she hadn't spent the night in the carnival house, if she hadn't pulled the stinger out of Damian's side, and if she hadn't been under attack by that thing, she would've thought she'd broken her mind. But as it was, she struggled up to standing and shouted.

"Help!"

Her cries for help only enraged his dragon further. It bellowed in anger the second its paws touched the earth, and the dragon's thoughts raced through Damian's mind.

This home was his home! And everything in it was his!

Including her!

Damian struggled to disconnect that thought from the dragon's mind; the girl was not part of the package—even if they were saving her. Damian knew he wasn't safe, and shit like this was why!

The tiger! Damian redirected, and the dragon growled.

Of course, the tiger. The dragon batted his concerns aside. He'd landed inside the circle it'd been creating of itself, trying to funnel her toward its face-bits, only she'd been smart enough not to run. He wove his head to look at her.

Stay here, he tried to emote, but with his dragon's face on, all snout and teeth, who the hell knew what she saw, or what she thought of him? Her eyes were wide, and she was terrified; he could smell it, but who wouldn't be?

Not me, Damian's dragon reminded him.

No, of course not, Damian groaned.

Never me. The dragon whirled, using his own Unearthly ability to hone in on the tiger's most solid part. *Because I like killing.*

The dragon pounced at this, using a massive paw to press half the tiger down, snapping its teeth through a portion of the rest of it. The problem with fighting a shimmer-tiger was the teleportation. If his dragon didn't kill enough of it, quickly, it'd vaporize itself, heal, and reform. So his dragon shook its head, feeling things snap and tear deliciously, clawing at the piece it'd bitten into until it was sure it'd rendered enough of the tiger's flesh useless that it could never regain its form.

At the end of it, he was spattered in acidic violet-colored blood—it streaked against his golden scales, and he resisted the urge to clean himself with his tongue.

See? the dragon rumbled, satisfied with itself. It whipped its head back and roared, a sound of ultimate triumph, arching its back and flexing its wings. *My home,* it insisted.

Yes, Damian agreed.

And now—my woman. The dragon's head snaked back to Andi with alacrity.

THAT...THAT *is a dragon.*

Her mind could barely name it; it felt so unreal. A lifetime of watching movies, reading books, playing video games, had somehow never prepared her to see the real thing. Had she hit her head when the van hit the fountain? Was this one more crazy thing here? Or was her mind cracking in two?

It was golden, massive, winged, and glorious—and it acted as if it could understand her. When it looked at her, Andi thought it was trying to communicate something, and for the first time that morning, she'd felt safe. But then it leapt onto the other beast, pressing it down with massive paws and slaughtered it in front of her. That was the only word that would work for what it did. She watched it snap its teeth through a chunk of the thing that hunted her and shake its head like a dog with a toy—between that and the keening sounds the other thing made as it died, she knew this moment would haunt her nightmares forever. Violet blood rained over the grounds as the feline demon was literally torn to meat in front of her.

But it was a *dragon.*

Saving her.

And when it was done, the dragon whipped its head back and roared, a sound of pure triumph, arching its back and flexing huge sail-like wings, until they blocked out the sun.

And then it turned to look at her.

Andi's heart had already been beating fast, but now it was as if she had shot herself with epinephrine.

The dragon folded its wings, lowering itself slowly as if trying not to scare her. And those eyes—those familiar eyes—they were massive now, but still the same.

Damian's eyes.

Damian was a dragon.

A real, honest-to-God dragon.

There are dragons in this world, my dear. Real dragons. Beware. To know a dragon is to be cursed.

But Grand Auntie Kim never explained how, exactly. And in the stories she'd told her, things weren't clear either. In some, the dragons were savage and ruthless; in others, noble protectors and guardians, but as she wracked her brain for childhood memories, she couldn't remember a way to tell one kind from the other. The only thing that echoed was Auntie Kim's warning about avoiding being cursed.

With what?

Why had I never bothered to ask her?

Because I didn't ever dare think they were real.

Yet Andi couldn't stop herself from moving toward the dragon, her hand outstretched.

She knew she would probably regret this later—but wouldn't she regret it just as much if she didn't? Which was worse? What ifs or never should haves?

She stopped mere inches away from him.

No! No, no, no! Damian shouted at the beast and fought to regain control from the inside. The dragon wrestled him.

Mine, it growled.

No. She is her own. Damian redoubled his efforts, pushing the dragon back and down.

For now, it conceded, and then abruptly went away, leaving Damian pushing against nothing but himself inside his dragon form.

Able for the first time to see the outside world with his own eyes, he found Andi.

Staring at him.

She knew what he was.

And still, she walked slowly toward him, with a look on her face that wasn't the horror, disgust, or fear he had expected.

It was awe.

She would turn and run at any moment, and he would have to chase her down, change back to human, and somehow convince her to go back to the house where he could expose her to the Forgetting Fire as quickly as possible.

But something in him wanted her to see this beastly part of him, the part he kept hidden deep inside. He folded his wings and lowered himself to all fours, in an attempt to make himself smaller and less threatening.

Step by slow step, she approached him, watching him as carefully as he was watching her. With his extended senses, he could hear the rapid beating of her heart, smell that sinfully sweet scent of near panic and wariness.

She stopped inches away from him.

Run, he thought, *run for your own good.*

He lowered his head to her, intending to show her his teeth, which were the size of short swords.

And to his surprise, she reached out and touched him.

I SHOULD RUN, she thought, *for my own good.*

But instead of running, she touched the protruding ridge on the side of the dragon's face, where a cheekbone would be on a human. His scales were hard and hot but not uncomfortably so.

Suddenly his scales rattled in a shivering reaction. Andi gasped and jumped back and watched as the dragon seemed to melt away.

And then Damian stood there, in human form. The same man

she'd seen in his bedroom earlier, only now completely naked, and the rest of him was just as hot as the half she'd already seen. He was perfectly proportioned chiseled perfection, and the memory of his lips on hers and his hands on her body came rushing back with fresh heat.

"Why aren't you afraid?" he asked her.

Andi blinked. "Should I be?"

Damian opened his lips, but no words came out. Instead, he tilted his head, watching her as if he thought she would bolt—running off screaming at any moment. She'd be lying to herself if she didn't admit that a small part of her wanted to do just precisely that.

Damian was a dragon. But he was also a man.

A very, very good-looking man. And the rest of her wondered if his skin would be as hot to the touch as the scales had if she felt it now.

Thoughts like that will only get me into trouble. Andi made an effort to look around, at the steaming bits of monster flesh scattered around them and the smoking wreck of a van behind her. She should be scared witless, and part of her was, but the same snark she hid fear with at the hospital came out to protect her. "I take it this is just another normal Friday night for you?"

"Saturday morning, technically," he corrected, slowly smiling.

She turned back toward him and smiled too, then quickly looked away—feeling her face getting red. She'd seen a lot of naked men; it was a hazard of her job, but he wasn't a patient, and...she tugged at the too long cuffs of the shirt she was wearing.

"So, what happened to your injury?" she asked.

He put his hand to his ribs where she'd pulled out the stinger. "I heal quickly."

"Uh-huh." She made every effort to keep her gaze high. "Any more monsters coming that I need to worry about?"

"Not to my knowledge." He kept looking at her strangely—like he thought she was the unreal one.

Andi folded her arms carefully. "Okay, then, look, are you going to tell me what's going on? Or are you going to pretend this isn't happening and tell me I'm going crazy?"

He squinted his golden eyes at her. "No. You're not going crazy," he said, tilting his head. "Aren't I...scary?"

The bubble of nervous expectation around her popped, and Andi laughed out loud. "If you have to ask, you're probably not." She gave up and let herself look at him, at his fucking perfect naked body. "At least, not right now."

He cracked a smile. "Yes, well, about that," he said, lowering his hands to cover himself politely, and then the smile fell from his face as he took a fast step toward her. "What's that?"

Andi blinked at his abrupt shift in tone. "What's what?"

He grabbed her arm and held it out. There was a spot of violet on the white shirt she was wearing, right under her left breast.

"Did it touch you?" He didn't unbutton it—he just grabbed both sides of it and ripped it off her.

CHAPTER NINE

Do not let anything happen to her! his dragon shouted at him, as though there was a chance in hell he might.

Shut it! he shouted back at it. He scooped her up as she shrieked, racing her back into the house and through the halls. How much Unearthly blood had touched her? How long had it been in contact with her skin? The closest earthly comparison was like phenol—an acid that numbed you as it burned—incredibly dangerous, and one of the many reasons all his men had magical protections.

"Damian!" She was pounding her fist on his chest, and he was entirely ignoring her until they reached the room with his dragon's bathing pond. He threw her far out into the water and then leapt into it himself to swim after her.

She bobbed back up, spitting water—and spitting mad. "What the fuck!"

"The blood is dangerous. You have no idea." He hauled her up to inspect her side.

"I'm half-naked!" she shouted at him.

"So? I'm all naked." He reached for her to inspect where the blood had brushed her skin. It had already erupted into a bright red welt. He dunked her back into the water, chest-height, and started swirling water quickly past it with a hand. She stood in the water on her tiptoes, panting angrily, water flowing over her breasts with each sweep of his hands, nipples pebbling in the pond's chill. *Shit.* "Grim, heat the pond!" he commanded.

"Do you want to explain what the fuck is happening to me right now?" She moved to cross her arms, to hide herself from him, but he caught her wrist just in time. He couldn't risk her getting burned elsewhere.

"I'm sorry. I know this is strange, but some Unearthly blood is acidic. Or poisonous. Depending on the monster."

Will she be all right? His dragon rushed forward inside him as if to see for himself.

STOP THAT, Damian commanded. Since when had his dragon ever given a fuck about a human?

Andi slowly lowered her head down to look at her side. "Don't," he warned her.

"I'm a nurse, okay? Let me see." She pushed his hands away and held her arm up, while holding her breast out of the way, rocking forward out of the water to look. Watching her touch herself, even for clinical reasons, did dark things to him. Damian wished the water was opaquer. "It doesn't look that bad," she went on.

"We caught it in time. But you'll need to stay in here for a while until it's all diluted—just in case."

She carefully crossed her arms high on her chest, fully covering herself from him. "Fine."

Had he been looking that greedily? If so, who was to blame? The remnants of the succubus's sting, his dragon, or him? All three? His dragon was roiling inside, beside himself with proprietary concern. He could still feel the surges of inappropriate lust—surely just his succubus-caused hangover from being attacked last night—and he'd be lying if he said she wasn't beautiful now. The perfection of her breasts, curve of her neck, the way her hair flowed around her like she was a goddamned mermaid, right down to the blue streak in it. After her kissing him earlier, it was all too easy to imagine them entwined together, his lips on her neck, her breasts pressed against him, his cock seated deep.

Yessssss, his dragon purred.

Damian quickly swallowed and splashed his face, trying to get his head clear. She would have to *forget* all this—he should not, could not get attached. It would only make it hurt more later.

Pain is fine, his dragon disagreed.

No one asked you, he told it.

ANDI WATCHED him splash himself beside her, totally in his element. Less than three minutes ago, she'd been flirting with a dragon, and now she was half-naked in the water with one. Oh, and also burned by acid from monster-blood—because that was a thing that could happen. And to think they never covered that in nursing school.

Damian dunked himself then resurfaced, snapping water out of his hair with a quick shake, before he looked at her again. She could tell by the way he was trying to look at her eyes and not down at all that he was trying very, very hard to grant her some privacy—and she was trying to do the same. Only the way his shoulders breeched the water and how she could see his biceps every time he moved his arms was pretty damn distracting—as was the rest of him. His wide chest narrowed down to abs that were as rippled as the water they both stood in—the expression on his face, dark and brooding like a storm. He was almost too hot to be real—which made sense because he was a dragon. A dragon. An actual, real, honest-to-God, wings-and-all dragon.

She let herself drop into the water, letting it surround her so that she could think. Then she made the mistake of opening her eyes and found herself at Damian's waist height—and the view below was not any less distracting than the view above. She sprang out of the water, back to her feet again.

If she slept with him—an "if" that was getting smaller all the time, turning the corner into a "when"—chances were, she would have a very good time.

"Are you okay?" He leaned closer, his voice full of concern. She had a feeling he was asking about more than the burn.

"Yeah. Why wouldn't I be? I just almost died two or three times, plus met a dragon. One that I kissed for some strange reason, earlier in the night." She laughed nervously and rose up on her tiptoes, the seam of his jeans riding uncomfortably-comfortable between her legs.

He grunted. "About that...that wasn't you."

"Tell me about it."

"No...literally. You weren't thinking right. You were under a spell."

Of course, she was, Andi thought with a titter. That made as much sense as anything else. She covered her breasts with her elbows and splashed her face with water to buy herself time to just calm down and think, because if she didn't, she was going to have a panic attack, or just sleep with him to stop from having one—because at the current rate of craziness, why not?—which also wasn't optimal. She released a breath and gathered herself before addressing him again. "So, you're going to tell me everything, right?" That was the least he could do after making her live through last night.

His eyes widened. "Not if I can help it." He looked away from her, a lock of dark wet hair falling into his face. "Andi, no one can know what we are. Or what we do."

She gave up on covering herself, as his words sank in. "Wait," she began, trying to manage this U-turn in her mind. "Why save me from getting burned if you're going to kill me?"

"What?" he whirled on her and laughed. "No. I'm not going to kill you."

His protest seemed genuine. "But you said—"

"No." He shook his head and grabbed her shoulders. And where she hadn't been able to feel the acid burning her before, she could feel him now, the heat emanating from his hands. She wanted to grab his wrists and pull them down around her. Was that really her or just his 'spell'? "You're safe with me. You're always safe with me. I swear. It's just that...you might not remember all this tomorrow."

She stepped back reluctantly. "And why is that?" Complicated emotions swam across his face, and it took him so long to answer, she made a guess. "You're cursed? And people forget you when they're not looking at you?" Was that what Auntie Kim had meant?

He barked a laugh. "I wish things were that easy. But no, there's a room here that I have to take you to before you leave. It'll help you forget things."

Andi double-blinked. "After everything I've seen? That seems incredibly unlikely."

He spread his hands into the water in front of her and bowed his head. "And yet, it's true."

Why had he told her?

Because he felt like he had to.

Because acting on anything he felt right now—no matter how badly he wanted her, without telling her—would've been fucked up. And there'd been a brief window when he could've been with her. Her body'd wanted him already; he could scent it this close to her—even in the water like they were—but he'd finally seen it in her eyes.

And so, he'd blurted the truth out to save her from himself. Now. While he was still strong enough. Before any of the things he ached for could happen.

Fool, his dragon chastised from a distance.

Damian closed his eyes and shook his head at his dragon and himself. Selflessness was not a trait often found in his family—or indeed, in any of the Unearthly—and it seemed to cost him more strength than his fire did. But his own mother had been lured in by some "situation" like this. He would never curse another woman to the life he'd watched her lead—one she'd had no choice in.

Meanwhile, Andi was talking at him. Peppering him with questions as her panic rose—*another way in which she is delicious*, his dragon noted—and he shook his head further.

"There's no point in explaining anything else," he said firmly, cutting her off mid-sentence. "More answers will only lead to more questions, and they're all a waste of time."

He looked down and saw the fear in her eyes—not quite wild, but getting there—and ignored the small dark voice in his head that said his dragon was right; her fear *was* beautiful and would that he could scare her more.

"You want me to forget me...you...this?" she sputtered, looking around the waters and then at him again. "No way."

"You have to. It's not safe."

"What about Austin?"

"He's different."

She crossed her arms again—this time defiantly and below her breasts—and it made him want to pick her up and bury his face in them.

Cut that out, he growled at his dragon.

You think that's me? his dragon laughed.

"I'm different!" she protested.

"You are." It was the truth. It had been a very long time since he'd allowed himself to think dark thoughts, and yet somehow, her presence summoned them. The things he could do to her if given time. All the ways he could make her scream. He swallowed, getting control of his urges. "Very different. And yet, all of this is way too dangerous for you."

"Why do you get to be the person to make that decision?"

"Because I'm the one who involved you in the first place." He advanced on her, slowly corralling her toward the shore. "You're less than twenty-four hours out from the only world you've always known. How terrible can it be to return?"

She stood her ground. "If you pick me up... If I am picked up by one more man today—I don't care what you can turn into—I am kneeing you in the balls. Which I have pretty good access to right now." She glanced down into the water pointedly.

At the thought of her fighting him, Damian bit back a smile. *She fights you because she wants you,* his dragon explained.

You have no idea how humans work, he explained back.

"It's just not safe for you to know, Andi. Humans shouldn't deal in Unearthly business. They wind up injured—like the man you cared for earlier tonight. And like you, here, now." He reached his hand out toward her rib cage, longing for an excuse to touch her again. "I don't want to pick you up and carry you to the Forgetting Fire. Don't make me."

He left his hand out and willed her to put hers inside of it. She hesitated, looking at him closely, searching for some mercy in his face. Finding none, she finally took his hand. He pulled her closer with it, and together they started walking back to shore.

W*HAT THE FUCK, what the fuck, what the fuck.* Andi's mind was spinning, looking for a way out. "And so we're both going to forget everything?" Andi picked the least bad option and tried to keep the fear out of her voice.

"No. Just you. I'm immune."

She stopped. "And, what, you'll just whisk me back to my apartment, with no explanation?"

"Pretty much. You'll wake up in bed and feel like you've been sick —it'll excuse the lost time." He lifted her hand out of the water like he was asking her to dance, propelling her forward again.

"And I won't remember being here?" How was such a thing possible? "What about taking the job?" She'd emailed herself a reminder! And it was in her personal calendar even—the old school one she kept in a notebook in her bag!

"Every remnant of me and this place in your memory will be erased."

"Then...how are you going to pay me?"

"There will be a bank error in your favor."

"How very Monopoly of you."

He snorted softly in response. They were both at waist height now, and she took the risk of looking over. *Goddamn.* Everything about him was amazing, and soon it wouldn't matter because of magic fire.

"Wait! What about the burn?" She pulled her hand out of his and twisted to see herself again. "Will that go away too?" He inhaled but didn't speak, and she squinted up at him. "It won't, will it? Because if you could magic it away, you would've just magically healed your friend." The longer he was silent, the more she knew that she was right. "So now you're going to put me back into the world with an unexplained scar? No."

"What do you mean, no? Andi—" he began.

"I mean, no." She backed into the water. Even if it was still cold and unforgiving—it was farther away from wherever it was that he wanted to take her. "Are you really going to fuck around in my head and erase my memories without my permission?"

"It's for your own good. I promise."

"Just the tip, right? Do you know how many times I've heard that one before?" She took a strong backstroke into the pool, farther away from him, and it was a shame he was being an asshole right now because he looked like a fucking Greek god. "No. I say no. I'll leave here—you'll definitely pay me—and I'll go home, and I'll never say another word about any of this to anyone. Your secret will be safe with me. But you're not messing with my mind." She was out where she'd begun now, where she could only barely touch the ground, sweeping her arms beside her to boost herself up.

He stared at her—through her, almost—like he was communing

with something inside himself. "You won't even remember," he finally said.

She stopped swimming and let herself sink, so the water brushed beneath her chin. He'd saved her life. He was a good person—dragon, whatever it was that he was—he had to be. So, she played her only card: "I may not remember it, but you will."

Either he would come out and swim after her and grab her...or.... She watched his face, trying to read him, wondering if she could really trust him even if he agreed not to erase her memories.

DAMIAN STOOD halfway in the water and watched her swim away. She had to know there was no way she could win a fight between them, and yet she wouldn't back down. Could he really go out there and drag her to shore, take her through his house screaming, and throw her in the room with the Forgetting Fire—even if it was for her own good?

He remembered the other side of his mother's history—a woman only a shell of herself—forced to forget parts of her past "for her own good" too many times.

"Fine," he said quietly. Her eyes widened, and she didn't move, not quite believing him.

"Promise it."

"My word is my word. You can take it or not," he said and turned to finish striding back to shore.

He heard her follow him, splashing in behind. He didn't bother to dry off—only yanked clothing out of his closet roughly. She caught up with him when he was half-dressed. Grimalkin had put a fresh replica of all her original clothing on his bed. He picked it up and tossed it to her the second she reached the door. She caught it, and he turned his back on her again.

"Interesting décor. You like to look at yourself a lot?"

Damian glanced up and saw himself in twenty different reflections. "Stop asking questions," he said, tucking in his shirt.

She was still afraid of him—he could tell by the way she skulked around the edges of the room, staying out of arm's reach, trying to find someplace to change where she wouldn't be reflected. Thank God all of the mirrors were closed right now. What would happen if his stepmother was looking through? She'd never let him live this down.

Or, she'd come here and kill Andi herself.

He ground his teeth together in frustration and looked back at her. "I'll be waiting outside. And if you touch anything in here, I can no longer guarantee your safety."

She nodded. Her long, wet hair had soaked through her shirt, clearly showing the nipples he'd seen earlier as if to torture him. "Understood."

He growled again, resisted the urge to pick things up and throw them, and went into the hallway, slamming the door behind himself.

You should never have told her, his dragon rumbled.

I'm different than you. And that's why I'm in charge.

For now. Now that there was no sex or violence in the offing, he felt his dragon's presence subside.

"Grimalkin meowed in this direction," Austin said, rising up the far stair and looking around. "Where's the girl?"

"Forthcoming," Damian said.

"As in, not unconscious?" Austin's head tilted like a particularly thoughtful hound. "Wait...what?"

"She's still her." For better or worse. Austin would find out momentarily, better to confess. He watched the other man smell the air. Damn him and his werewolf nose.

"And...you didn't sleep with her?"

"No."

Austin worked his jaw several times before speaking again. "I'm just having a hard time figuring out how this happened."

"I'll save you time. She's her own person, and I am unconscionably unlaid." Damian ran a hand back through his wet hair. "Do you mind taking her home? It's been a rather long night. Or...maybe Mills?" His secretary wouldn't be happy as a chaperone, but she would be a whole lot less threatening than Austin to the girl after this morning. "And how is your brother? Did he make it through the night all right?" He didn't need rest so much as he just needed to be away from Andi. The faster he could throw himself back into his work, the faster he could push everything that happened tonight into the past. He knew Jamison had gotten good data off of their last gate, so at least Zach's injury hadn't been for nothing. And if they could just predict the next one's arrival and seal it before it opened, none of his people would get hurt again.

"Mills isn't up yet." Austin eyed him warily again. "And Zach's fine...but are you?"

Andi's arrival interrupted any response. She stepped out into the hallway tentatively, fully dressed down to her coat, which was zippered and buckled up to her neck. It didn't matter though, parts of him had already memorized how she looked, she could never truly hide from him again. Austin looked between them and made a shoving gesture. "We could still—"

Andi caught Austin's meaning and stepped quickly behind Damian.

"He's taking you home," Damian said, sidestepping to reveal her.

"Am I going to be safe with him? He's not going to try to make me forget, is he?" she asked him, without taking her eyes off of Austin.

"You'll be as safe as you are with any of my men."

"After last night, that's not comforting."

Damian closed his eyes. He didn't have time for this. It had caught him off guard how hard the human half of him experienced the strange shining moment of hope he'd had with her earlier—and how hard it was to extinguish now, crushing it back into his dark heart like a spent cigarette. "Look, I could've just picked you up, thrown you into the room, and closed the door."

"But you didn't because you're not an asshole."

He whirled on her. "You don't really know what I am." He grabbed her shoulders with both hands, turned, and propelled her toward Austin. "Go! Now! And never speak of this again!"

He watched her open her mouth—and he wasn't sure if she would fight or agree—when a distant alarm started beeping, somehow stopping her. Concern flashed across both her and Austin's faces. They looked at each other as the sound continued, found confirmation in one another's expression, and both started racing downstairs.

Unsure what was going on or what they'd find, Damian raced after them.

CHAPTER
TEN

Andi knew an oxygenation alarm meant one of two things: a patient was scratching themselves and messing up the sensor, or they were decompensating—possibly dying. She reached the bedside a half second after Austin, who for once seemed totally stunned. He was mesmerized by the screen's report of dropping numbers, turning white as a sheet.

She whirled and pounded her fists on his chest. "Get it together! Where's your ambu bag? And your O2 tank?"

Her violence startled him to activity. He cursed and ran off for the crash cart he'd apparently put away. Andi looked around. If this house was as magic as she thought, couldn't it just conjure things up? The cat ran in and looked at her expectantly—as did Damian.

"What's going on?" he asked, his concern written all over his face. She ignored him.

"Suction?" she asked aloud, and heard something large land behind her. She turned and found an entire suction set up—canister, tubing, and all—and heard its portable generator start to whine. *This house!* She grabbed the end of the tube and stuck it into the patient's mouth, hoping that if there was something in there blocking his throat, it'd suck it out. His saturation was in the seventies. If Austin didn't hurry up....

At that moment, Austin raced in, shoving the cart ahead of him. He laced the oxygen tubing between the portable tank and the ambu bag that they'd start to use to breathe for the patient—if it worked. "Catch!" he said, throwing the ambu bag at her after it was attached.

She tossed the suction aside—it hadn't seemed to help—and she put the mouthpiece around the patient's mouth, jerking his chin up to clear his airway, and started squeezing. He was getting 100% oxygen now. If he was going to get better, now was the time to do it—and if this didn't work... Andi looked back at Austin. "When's the last time you intubated anybody?"

"Been a while," he admitted, ripping through the crash cart drawers for the intubation kit.

"Grab the defibrillator pads while you're there," she told him. The patient's oxygenation saturation was at 60% now—soon, the cells of his heart would start freaking out about not getting enough air.

Damian shoved forward. "What's going on?" he demanded.

"You sure you're not a doctor?" Andi said, as sarcastically as possible. "Get out of the way," she said, shoving at his hips with her own. He danced aside, and she yanked off the sheet she'd placed over the patient's freshly-dressed chest in between squeezing the ambu bag.

His heart rate shot up, setting a different monitor blaring.

"Pads! Pads! Pads!" she shouted as Austin reached over to slap them on.

And then Damian grabbed her wrist. "Get back."

She twisted to look at him in annoyance. "I am *breathing* for him. Until Austin hurries his ass up—"

He grabbed her shoulders and picked her up to set her behind him. "Fucking stop doing that!" she yelled and punched his arms.

Everyone's ability to pick her up any time they wanted to was entirely unfair.

But Austin was stepping away as well, his hands reaching behind him for a holstered gun she hadn't clocked earlier.

"What?" she asked again, more quietly, stepping out from behind Damian where he'd placed her.

The men were watching something underneath the dressing on the patient's chest surge—like a wandering hand.

"You've gotta be fucking kidding me," Austin said. "Reinforcements!" he shouted to the room at large, although Andi had no idea what or who was listening.

"Back! Back! Back!" Damian said, and she knew from his gestures he meant her. Grimalkin's ears flattened as he joined their line, hissing at the bed.

Andi swallowed. *What...on...Earth...* She realized then that the phrase *Unearthly* was right.

The dressing peeled aside and a small hand—a goddamned hand, although it had talons on the ends of each finger—reached out.

Another well-armed stranger ran into the room, as what was in the man's stomach pulled itself out, bracing itself against his pelvis as it wriggled free.

Why aren't you shooting? she wanted to scream—because what she was watching was so improbable it was bending her mind. The child-sized creature was all the shades of blue, covered in mucus; its face was missing eyes, and she could count its teeth at twenty feet. But below it, their friend was still—somehow—alive, or so the monitor claimed.

"Take it when you've got it," Damian commanded as a darkskinned man came in. He was wearing an armature across both shoulders to brace a silver weapon, and he had a sight-piece folded out in front of one eye.

"Charging!"

There was a high-pitched whine, and Austin looked warily at his comrade. "If you so much as singe a hair on my brother, Jamison," he warned, his voice low.

The man with the gun nodded. "Understood. Firing!"

For a long second, nothing happened. And then what she could only describe as a beam of blindingly red light flashed out of the gun—turning it for a moment into almost a light saber—and it clipped the creature.

The monster screamed and jumped up to the ceiling, revealing a long tail behind it—how was it possible that entire thing was inside her patient?—then it started skittering toward them like a spider, making horrible sounds. She dropped down, covering her ears and shrieking as the thing's mouth opened and a tongue as long as its tail dropped out, lashing toward the man with the weapon. Austin started emptying his handgun into it, while Damian shouted, "Jamison!" and bringing out a gun of his own.

"Charging!" the other man shouted back, and again that high-pitched whine. Andi fell to her knees—all the better to hide from whatever the fuck was happening, anything to get away from her rising sense of terror.

And then the patient's monitor began beeping ominously. A small geyser of red started shooting out of the hole the monster'd left behind—a severed artery. The monster was swiping at them, swinging from the ceiling like some demented spider-creature, leaping from bookcase to bookcase—its tail and tongue swirling around it. They tried to take shots without hitting one another in the enclosed space, waiting for the laser beam weapon to charge, and then it ran across the ceiling into a hall.

"Goddammit!" Damian cursed.

"Stay human!" Austin shouted. The three of them chased after it, followed closely by the cat.

"Grimalkin!" Damian shouted, but his castle's avatar was already on it, rearranging the house's alignment so the hallway they were in connected with an empty garage—an almost smooth cube of a place, with no furniture to hide behind. The lurker ran in—dodging shots from Austin's gun—snaking up and down the wall. Damian lined up beside Jamison, ready to protect the man from the monster as he readied his weapon. "Why's it taking so long?" Damian demanded.

"I'm charged, but I've gotta wait for the barrel to cool down so the metal won't deform."

"That's unacceptable," Damian growled.

"It's physics!" Jamison shrugged, making the armature around him bob. "I'll work out a way to cool it off, next rev—now that we know that it works."

Damian grunted. Jamison's weapon was the runner-up project to gate sealing and the culmination of years of high-level experiments on killing Unearthly creatures. Because if they couldn't get ahead of the gates opening, the next best solution was to be able to obliterate whatever came through from the other side. The knowledge that there was only one of him and a near-infinite amount of Unearthly ready to pour through if the gates ever stayed open weighed on him —just as he knew it did the other gatekeepers. If they could finally get it right—get it down to a one-shot, one-kill situation—then he would never have to worry about someone else getting hurt like Michael or Zach again. But what the fuck had *happened* to Zach? How the hell had the lurker gotten in?

"Ready!" Jamison shouted, kneeling down for a better shot. The lurker reached the end of the garage and twisted back—looking for an escape—and then all three men watched the creature disappear.

It didn't evaporate entirely, but it changed all of its colorations to merge perfectly with its surroundings, and since everything in the room but them was a sterile-white, it was impossible to see. "Grim!" Damian shouted, jumping in front of his people, letting his dragon rise up inside.

Ceiling, left, his dragon noted, then strained against his will. *Free me*, it commanded.

"Upper left," Damian grunted, holding his dragon back with a, *No*. "Quickly," he warned his men.

Jamison and Austin did as they were told, as Grimalkin paused behind. A door to the left opened up, summoned by the housecat, and swung open loudly. Damian saw the ripple of the lurker running out against its trim. Jamison took his shot—and a good patch of the ceiling. But no blue creature appeared in the falling rubble.

"Fuck! Where next?" Austin shouted, running in.

"Charging!" Jamison said, heading right after.

The men ran after it, and Damian had no doubt that Grimalkin had sent them into a room with better visibility. He ran for the door as well.

His dragon chose then to attack. *Free me!* it demanded, struggling to take over. Damian caught himself against the door's side and held a fist to his stomach.

This was the real reason they needed the weapon.

Because someday the dragon in him would escape, and he wouldn't be able to fold it back inside himself again.

"Cut it out!" he growled and ran after his men.

ANDI WONDERED MOMENTARILY where the house would take them, and then she ran for the bed. The center of her patient was open and raw and flooding with blood, but he was breathing now, so that was good, at least? If somehow birthing whatever-the-fuck that thing was hadn't killed him, she'd be damned if he died now.

She balled up the remains of the dressing from earlier up in her hands and leaned into the wound and would've sworn she saw something inside of him shimmer like a mirror for a second before bloody cotton covered it up.

A lot of things glistened inside people—under the right light—though. When you didn't have the right words on hand, you reached for metaphors. She'd seen lung tissue flutter like butterfly wings and exposed fat that looked like pillow stuffing. Whatever it was, she knew one thing, that if she stopped applying pressure and keeping what little blood the man had left inside him and circulating, he would die. His death was not worth her curiosity.

She leaned harder, putting her whole weight into him, replacing her hands with elbows, until she could get enough leverage on the bed to clamber onto it so that she could kneel over him, pressing down on him like she could push death itself away if she only tried hard enough.

And then there was a scrabbling behind her. She could hear shouts, hissing, the shots of a gun. Movement burst into the room, something running across the ceiling that she knew she didn't want to see, and tumult behind her.

"Andi, get down!" Damian shouted. But she knew if she did, the man would bleed to death. "NOW!"

Andi ducked but didn't move. She felt the swipe of a tongue sweep across the back of her neck and the hot breath of whatever it was that'd escaped. She closed her eyes and prayed not to die.

"Girl, stay down! Eyes closed!" the dark-skinned man commanded. It looked like one of his arms was entirely metal? *But how?* Andi did as she was told, and then she heard the strange charging whine sound of the monstrous gun that he wore. A burst of energy shot over her head, light flooded into her eyes—even through her closed eyelids—and an inhumane squeal started and ended abruptly as something wet and disgusting fell onto her, knocking her farther into her patient's guts, before sliding off her back to land on the hardwood floor with a thump.

The lurker was dead—no thanks to him—and Damian ran forward, ready to lift Andi off of Zach. Blood covered her from her hands up to her elbows, and the blue grease of the lurker slicked her now from the top down. He could read the anger and fear on her face where he could see it between her wet locks of hair and watched those attributes merge into a magnificent ferocity that drew him to it like a flame.

"Come down off of there at once!" he commanded, reaching for her.

She made a sound at him—a snarl—that clearly meant get away. "If I move, he'll bleed out and die."

He looked to Austin for confirmation of this fact. He was ripping through the drawers of the cart he'd wheeled into the room—a lifetime ago, it seemed—opening the plastic wrapped IV bags with his teeth before hanging them and squeezing them with his own two hands so that the fluids inside them would rush into Zach more quickly.

Andi watched Austin with wide eyes. "What the fuck are you doing? You have to call 911!"

"No!" Austin shouted. "He can handle it."

"He doesn't need fluids! He needs blood!"

Austin flung his arms wide. "How the fuck would we explain this to anyone?"

"Do you want your brother to die or not?"

And then both of them looked to Damian for a decision. "Call 911," he commanded.

"D...we can't trust hospitals. You know that. And...this is going to get us crushed..." Austin pleaded.

"I'd do no less for you," he said with a tone that broached no discussion. "Keep him alive until they get here."

"Fuck both of y'all," Austin muttered, looking between him and the girl, but he reached for his phone and dialed.

Damian turned to Jamison, who was practically dancing with excitement. "It worked! I knew it!"

"It did," Damian said. Just like he'd wanted it to—just like he'd paid for.

His young techmaster inhaled to say something else, but his eyes flashed over to Andi first.

"Whatever you want to say, say it," Damian said, studiously not looking at Andi himself. The less he thought about her, the better; he already had far too much on his mind.

Jamison ducked over to where the girl couldn't see him, eclipsed by Damian's larger presence. "We, uh, still need to test it on bigger creatures. Just to be certain."

Code-words for: *Will this really kill me?* Damian knew. His dragon growled a challenge inside him, from where he'd hidden it away.

Damian nodded. "Indeed."

Austin finished his phone call and was loudly discussing what to do next with Andi, the monitor was beeping incessantly. Grimalkin was pacing from wall to wall, hissing disapproval at so much destruction in his house, and Jamison had pulled out some sort of half-divining-rod-half-game-controller-like device to wave over the lurker's corpse.

Damian toed it, watching a tentacle-like arm flop while grinding his teeth together. How the hell had it gotten in? What if he hadn't been there? And the gun hadn't worked?

Could he have lost all of them?

He looked over to where Andi was, appearing largely unfazed despite being covered in body fluids, talking loudly to Austin about what she thought would help next.

Could he have lost...her?

He kicked the lurker in earnest and watched it slide across his floor, into a door Grimalkin conveniently opened and then closed, making its corpse disappear. "We also need to solve the question of how the fuck a portal opened endangering everyone IN MY CASTLE."

He hadn't meant to shout the last three words, and yet he had. Everyone else in the room snapped to silence, except for the monitor.

See? his dragon laughed at him. *You can't even control yourself. How can you hope to ever control me?*

That's what the gun is for, Damian snarled back.

You wouldn't dare, the dragon challenged.

Try me.

But instead of surging up to wrestle, his dragon roiled back inside him, feeling suffused with mirth. Damian inhaled and exhaled slowly as Jamison stood.

"I'll have to get back to you on that," he said and went to run his gizmo over Zach's body on the bed. And there, despite his best efforts not to, Damian's eyes met Andi's.

Whatever else was happening at that moment fell away. All the noise and commotion seemed to hush, and it was just him and her—a dragon-shifter and a gore-covered goddess.

Are you okay? he mouthed at her, unable to imagine that she could be.

Her eyebrows rose, betraying the utter absurdity of the question given the situation, and a sarcastic smile played at the edges of her lips.

Fuck, no, she mouthed back at him. *But I'm all right.*

He wanted to lunge in, grab her, and swoop her up, to take her someplace far away from here. But before he could even think to act, a group of uniformed men was clattering in behind a gurney.

"What the fuck happened here?" one of them asked.

ANDI WATCHED with increasing disbelief as Damian explained his friend's wounds away as tiger disembowelment—and Grimalkin changed his form into one, going from a small Siamese into a three hundred pound black and orange striped beast in half a second.

"Fuck!" one of the paramedics shouted, spotting him.

"Run along, Stripey," Damian told the tiger, and it did. "He's usually very well behaved," Damian told the paramedics. "You'll find we have the appropriate wildlife permits."

The rest of everything was explained—somehow—by Austin's training and their quick thinking. Of course, they'd intubated the man. Of course, they'd put IVs into him. Of course, an eccentric billionaire would have all the tools and equipment for keeping himself alive nearby—of course, of course, of course. But the absent Mr. Blackwood "senior," she pieced together from overhearing their story, wasn't here presently—also, of course. He was off doing business in Dubai. She overheard Damian give the paramedics his own name though as Damian Blackwood the Third—the elderly billionaire's "useless" younger cousin, according to her pre-job internet searches.

Listening in, Andi had a strong nursing hunch that Mr. Blackwood "senior" didn't actually exist.

"We've got him, Miss," one of the paramedics said, placing his hands over hers, preparing to take over pressure-duties.

"Really?" she asked, then shook her head at herself. She could barely handle what had happened; there was no need to tell anyone else about things. Andi pulled her hands back like she was doing a magic trick and dismounted the bed. The rest of the paramedics buckled him in, and she thought to ask, "Where are you taking him?"

"General," the medic closest to her answered.

Another of them said at her expression, "Don't worry, it's a trauma center. They've seen worse."

She already knew that. General was her home away from home. Her last shift seemed so long ago, and her next shift—fuck, no. She was calling in sick tonight. She'd been awake for over twenty-four hours, had had her life threatened at least twice, and had met a real-life dragon. A girl needed time to adjust.

"Hey," Damian said from beside her. Austin was trailing after the men. She had a feeling he'd cop a ride in the ambulance, the stranger-with-the-metal-arm was gone as was the magic-cat, and something had happened to the blue-monster-thing when she hadn't fully been paying attention.

"There's not an older version of you running all this somewhere, is there," she stated flatly.

He shrugged, not looking caught in the least. "No. Whenever we need the 'elder' Blackwood to go out, we slap some magic on my friend whose life you just saved, and he pretends to be an older version of me."

"Why?"

"Because that way, everyone pays attention to him, and no one gives a shit about me." His voice held a deep tone of irony as he went on. "Everyone knows I'm just the asshole. Go ask Google."

Andi felt her eyebrows rise. Damian was the asshole who was also a dragon who had saved her life—before threatening to erase her memories. She looked up at him and caught him staring at her again—probably afraid she'd tell someone his secret—and she suddenly felt swamped by exhaustion. "Take me home?"

He nodded quickly. "Of course."

TOGETHER THEY WALKED to the front of the house and out the main door. The fountain was fixed. The van had disappeared. And now they were heading toward a garage—not the one she'd wrecked before—and Damian used his handprint to unlock it. The white door rose up, revealing the sleekest looking car she'd ever seen inside, low-slung and gold, as shiny as an icicle. She didn't recognize the make, but she saw the logo on the side.

"Pagani?" she asked aloud.

Damian snorted. "It means expensive, in Italian." He moved to hold a winged door open for her, and she looked down at herself.

It was at this point she realized she was in shock. Because normal Andi would've never stood for this, being covered in human blood—and who knew what else from that monster-thing—down to her toes, definitely under her fingernails. Normal Andi would've been finding a vat of alcohol sanitizer to bathe in. As it was, she just asked, "And your expensive upholstery?"

He shrugged with a small smile. "It's seen worse."

She didn't fight him on this. She just sank inside and let the buttery leather interior catch her, putting her seat belt on and curling up into a ball against the door. A pierced golden coin hung from his rearview mirror on a satin ribbon instead of fuzzy dice—because of course it did. She watched it sway back and forth as he drove and she let the hypnotic motion of it lull her into sleep.

CHAPTER
ELEVEN

By the time Damian pulled into the parking lot of her apartment complex, she was sound asleep. He thought about waking her, then hesitated. He told himself that she needed to sleep—she was mortal, that he was doing her a favor—but he knew the truth. He was afraid if he woke her up, it would be the end. She would want to shower, of course. She'd get out of his car, take the cash, and leave. Why wouldn't she, after everything he'd put her through last night? And there was nothing that he could or should do to make her stay. Her leaving was the right choice.

Unless it wasn't.

He looked over at her, curled up into her seat with her seat belt still on. She hadn't been scared of him as a dragon at all. He remembered the look on her face seeing him—awestruck, but as she raised her hand, also certain. Like she knew she belonged with him.

No. That was just the loneliness talking. He could never wish being with him on anyone. The coin Michael'd given him hung on a ribbon around his rearview mirror. It was bad enough that Austin and the rest of them had been dragged into working with him; being on his crew had cost Michael his life.

So he would never dare to bring someone so soft and fragile into the Realm of the Unearthly, but he watched her chest rise and fall and listened to the quiet sounds of her breathing—remembering the way she'd looked at him as a man when they'd been in the pond. He would have sworn there'd been a moment or two there where she'd felt his pull and had wanted him alike.

Which didn't matter. One of them had to be the strong one. And just because she didn't want to forget things didn't mean she wanted a relationship with him. Who could—fully knowing what he was? So, any minute now, he would wake her up, shove an envelope of cash at her, and push her out of the car.

She stirred against the leather seat and made a small noise. She would be so much more comfortable in her own bed after a shower, no doubt. All the more reason he should wake her. *Yes, be an adult about this already.* He steeled himself, reaching over, but before he could touch her, need wracked him as it never had before, making him stop, and he slowly closed his hand. He almost didn't trust himself. For all the times he'd touched her already, he wanted more. At the least, he didn't want this to be the end—like it would be if he woke her.

And what was the rush? Austin had already texted him that Zach was critical but stable—his werewolf abilities serving him in good stead. The full moon would come tonight and heal him. So, couldn't he just sit here and pretend she was choosing to be with him for a little bit longer?

Why did she have to be perfect? There were a million ways she could've acted differently today and turned him off, but somehow, she'd navigated every one. And that last vision of her atop Zach, saving his life, so impossibly brave despite its absolute utter foolishness—he'd never seen such ferocious selflessness before.

Whereas, everything about him and his desires *was* selfish—born from a place of dragonhood, where what he wanted, he got. Which was why he was watching her take the world's most uncomfortable nap in his sports car, after the fucking worst night he'd had since Zach had gotten injured.

Goddamn it. Just touch her. Just wake her up.

As if his own desires made it manifest, she inhaled deeply, and her eyes blinked. She startled, looking at him, and then around at the car, as her hands reached for the door. "Oh my God...oh...wait...what..." she began, and he realized if only he'd been sly enough to somehow get her into a shower and into her bed without waking her—or doing anything lewd—she might've decided everything that'd happened to her was a dream, even without the fire.

"You," she said slowly, her eyes finding his.

"Me," he agreed. What did she remember? What was she thinking of him?

You soft, scaleless fool, his dragon chided from a distance. *Who cares? Take what you want.*

"You're...a dragon."

"Yes." No point in denying it now.

"Just...like Auntie Kim..." she breathed, making no sense, before going to rub an eye with the back of one hand and realizing it was still gross from earlier. "Ewww." Then she looked around again and squinted through the tinted windows at the sun. "What time is it?"

He glanced at his phone. "Eleven."

"I've been asleep for three hours?"

Had it really been three hours? Damian realized, not for the first time, that no one else was better at torturing himself than he was. "Not long enough."

"And...you've just been watching me?"

"Mostly day trading," he lied, flashing her his phone.

She stretched like a cat and looked around at herself again. "I can't believe you didn't wake me up."

"I didn't want to touch you..." which was even more of a lie before he quickly added, "...without your permission."

"So, non-consensual brainwashing was okay, but a shoulder tap's right out? Good to know." She snorted at him before her lips curved into a smile. It was just as warm as he remembered from the night prior and before he could sensibly stop himself, he was smiling back.

"I don't really have a rulebook for this," he admitted.

"This?" she asked, her eyebrows arching.

What he wanted to say was, *You, me, sitting in a car, me wanting more, do you want more with me?* But what he said instead was, "Interacting with humans."

She looked a little wounded at that, and he wished he hadn't said anything at all. "Are we really all that different?"

"I don't know. I've never been human before." *Why wasn't she running?*

"But, you hang out with them, I met people—"

"Most of them are supernatural in some way." *Did she want to stay, too?*

"Unearthly?" she guessed, remembering.

"Hmmm. Not entirely. More like offshoots of Unearthly creatures from generations ago. Been on Earth so long that they're different now; I don't think they could really function in the Realms anymore."

She eyed him warily. "I thought you didn't want me asking questions?"

"I haven't told you a single thing that you could actually Google," he said.

She frowned, and he realized it was only her curiosity that kept her here. *Of course. Grow up, Damian.* He sat up straight and gave her a predatory smile. *Leave little girl, get out of my car; run away before I hurt you.* She read his face and stiffened but didn't reach for the door, and he spotted the envelope sitting between their car seats. "Here," he said, picking it up and tossing it into her lap. "I tripled your fee. Hazard pay, after last night." Now she would be sure to go.

She stared at the fat envelope without touching it.

"What's wrong?" he asked.

"This…just…it feels like a bribe." She shoved at the envelope with a finger.

He blinked at her. "You did a job. You need the money."

She looked over at him, eyes flashing—he'd clearly struck a nerve. "I guess I do. I guess people like me get bought by people like you." She grabbed the envelope and reached for the door, and he ought to have just let her leave, but he couldn't help but protest.

"That's not what I meant," he said, grabbing her wrist before she could go. "I mean, of course, we did a background check on you—"

Andi shook him free but settled down. "And that's better?" she asked, holding her wrist where he'd touched it.

"I was leaving you in a room with my best friend and about ten thousand dollars' worth of narcotics. Forgive me for not being trusting."

He couldn't read the emotions flowing across her face. Pride was one of them, he was sure—beautiful and misplaced—but she was also breathing heavy, and she still wasn't leaving, despite his semi-best efforts to get her to go.

If she really wanted to leave, wouldn't she have left already?

Her hand curled around the envelope as though she were considering it, but then she asked, "Is he all right?"

"Yes. Because of you."

She nodded. "That's good."

"It is," he agreed.

Silence passed between them then—far too long to not be noticed by both. "So, I guess this is it, isn't it?" she asked him, her voice small—asking him for permission to leave and acknowledgement that it was over.

Neither of which were things he had to grant.

Blood rushed in his ears like static and ran other places far more dangerous. A distant part of him realized that if he were a dragon now, she would be the size of one delicious bite precisely.

He both knew what he ought to tell her and what he wanted to.

"It should be," he said carefully.

Should was a pregnant word. It had room in it. It was an acknowledgement that telling her anything else was a bad idea, that his mere presence in her life would only bring danger into hers. But it wasn't a closing door.

Did it make him less of a man, being unable to walk away?

Or was this the most human thing he'd ever done?

"Should?" she asked as if tasting the opportunity.

"Should," he repeated.

If she was smart enough for both of them, if she got out and slammed the door behind herself, he would be strong enough not to follow her. Instead, he watched her open up the door, step out, and look back in at him.

"And...what happens if it's not the end?" she asked, as the predator in him heard her pulse speed up.

Damian let go of a breath, and a fresh match struck against the dark roughness of his heart and burst into flame. "Then, you text me with a date and time, and I'll come flying, so to speak."

A smile teased around the edges of her lips but didn't quite escape. "Okay." She nodded and carefully closed the car's door. He watched her hair swirl around her and her ass sway as she took the stairs up to her apartment over the bakery, and he waited until she'd safely unlocked her door and walked inside before turning the key in the ignition.

Mine, his dragon claimed her. *Just like I told you.*

Shush, he told the beast, but he didn't deny it.

CHAPTER
TWELVE

No sooner had Andi closed her apartment door behind her, then her phone started to buzz.
You are so, sooooooooooooo busted.
Girl, get right back down here. I need you to try a new thing!
Don't think I didn't see you!
Eumie—her close friend and the owner of the bakery downstairs—was blowing up her phone. Andi groaned and turned around. *I'll violate about forty different health codes if I come inside,* Andi texted back, as she walked down the stairs.
Alley! Now! Eumie demanded.
Andi sighed and doubled back beneath the stairs to take the narrow pathway behind the building on the right-hand side until she was behind the bakery, where Eumie could sneak out.
The scent of cinnamon, vanilla, and sugar wafted from the kitchen, overwhelming the typical alley smells. Eumorphopoulo—aka Eumie—was in their fifties and had that smooth Mediterranean light brown skin that was sometimes mistaken for a deep tan. They were non-binary and their gender presentation was fluid, but today they had on big gold hoop earrings, which Andi had learned for them

was femme. "Okay, what on God's green half-acre were you doing getting out of Damian Blackwood the Third's fancy ass vehicle?" Eumie started talking before she'd even cleared the door. Then they took all of Andi in. "And why the hell did he take you to play paintball?"

She looked down at herself, still covered in blue splotches. It was the most reasonable explanation. "It...was a long night."

Eumie's arms crossed as they gave Andi *the look*. Eumie was short, and their green bakery apron hung down almost to their feet like a wide snake's tail. Their bright beady eyes missed nothing, which usually made them an excellent friend/maternal-substitute-material, except for situations like right the fuck now.

"What did you want me to try?" Andi asked quickly, trying to deflect and noting the slice of bread in Eumie's hand. "You're going to have to feed it to me; I'm absolutely disgusting." "Fine, missy," Eumie said, holding it out for Andi to take an obliging chomp.

It was...delicious. Like pho, only in bread form. "Oh my God, Eumie...that's magical." She had to fight to stop for reaching for the rest of the slice. "It's just like my grandmother never made."

Eumie preened a little, although Andi knew she still wasn't out of the question zone. "Basil transcends all culinary borders," Eumie said, then tossed the rest of the slice over Andi's shoulder for the pigeons, and Andi knew her chance to dodge was over. "Okay, so, now that we've both acknowledged I'm a baking genius...what the hell?"

"Would you believe I can't tell you anything about it because of patient privacy?" Andi said, searching for cover. Eumie snorted like they didn't believe her—usually, Andi stopped in and unwound at the bakery after a shift, before going upstairs and sleeping. "I mean, how do you even recognize his car anyways?"

"Because I keep waiting for the chance to key it," Eumie said matter-of-factly, and Andi knew they weren't lying. Eumie donated baked goods to every nonprofit under the sun and had run for city council more than once on a platform of anti-gentrification—

whereas Damian's family's public face was pretty much gentrification personified. Eumie must've seen some of Andi's discomfiture in her expression because they then said, much kindlier, "He is really good-looking though. He's a useless spoiled roustabout—but a handsome one."

She bit her lips and looked down at her phone with his contact information in it—Damian's offer to fly to her still ringing in her mind. "Good-looking enough that you wouldn't hate me for going out with him?" she asked, wincing.

"Oh," Eumie said, everything about them softening. "So, it's like that, is it?"

"I don't know what it's like yet," Andi said truthfully.

"Well, I guess that depends on if he's going to keep trying to tie-dye you," Eumie said, giving Andi's current state of blueness a meaningful glance. "But...just because I'm opposed to him politically doesn't mean that you shouldn't have a little fun." Eumie held up their thumb and forefinger an illustrative amount, spreading them apart slowly as they talked. "And if you talk to him about spending some of his immense wealth on something other than a ridiculous sports car, the homeless shelter on Fifth and Grand has got it rough."

Andi's eyebrows rose. "Do you want me to be Robin Hood, or are you whoring me out?" she teased.

"It's a fine line, is all I'm saying." Eumie closed their eyes and raised their hands up into prayer, intoning like a yoga instructor during Shavasana. "Go where the vagina takes you. You only live once." And then they winked open one sly eye. "But if your vagina takes you into a billionaire's mansion, you should definitely steal some shit. It's not like he'll know."

"Eumie!" Andi protested.

"What?" Eumie answered with a straight face, before snickering into laughter.

"You know what!" Andi said, laughing along. "I'm dying. You've killed me, so I'm dead. No more about my vagina—"

"And speaking of dead things," Eumie said, giving Andi a knowing look.

"Oh. My. God!" Andi sputtered. "You're lucky I love you!"

"I am!" they agreed. "But it's time you took down that shrine to Josh up in there. He couldn't handle you because he didn't deserve you. So, flip the sign between your legs from closed to open. You're too young for that nonsense," Eumie said, waving her away with both hands. "Go have fun. Even if it is with the devil."

Andi grinned at her friend, trying to keep her thoughts off her face as her heart beat quickly.

He's not a devil.

He's a dragon.

ANDI CREPT BACK up her stairs to her apartment, closing the door gently behind herself and quietly taking off her shoes, hoping beyond hope that she could dodge Sammy until she got into her shower.

"Hi! I'm alive! Going to sleep now!" she announced the second her hand was on her bedroom door handle, and she heard Sammy's sleep-muffled response as she darted inside. She braced herself against her bedroom door, happy to see her normal things again. Her cheap red rug peeking around the edges of her bed made with cotton penguin-patterned sheets. Her secondhand chair covered in clothes she hadn't bothered to put away. Her desk covered with books and bills and a treasured family portrait of the three of them—her, her brother, and mom, all smiling at her dad who'd been taking the picture—but it was just as well he wasn't in the photo now. To the left was a small bookshelf with even more books on it. More than a few of them had dragons in them and *what the hell did they know!* To the right was a floor-length mirror so she could check herself over before going out. A framed *Fast and the Furious* poster Sammy'd given her was on one wall in lieu of any real art. Sammy had pried it off her own bedroom wall to give to her when Josh had bailed because she needed better men—like Vin Diesel and the Rock—in her life, even if they were unattainable, except for in her imagination.

And thinking of imaginary things—the wheels that'd been propelling her forward fell off, and her mind started to spiral.

Everything Grand Auntie Kim had told her was true! He'd seen her naked—and she'd seen him naked—and she'd seen him with wings and scales because he was *a dragon! A freaking dragon!*

The knowledge of what he was and what had happened had been bouncing around inside her head like a pinball ever since she'd woken up inside his car. He'd saved her life—more than once—but he was *a dragon, a dragon, a dragon!* Some primal, frightened part of her kept shouting. But he didn't look like one just minutes ago—completely human and covered in the same mess she was—although somehow, he'd worn it better, which was completely unfair.

What would Auntie Kim say now, if she were still alive? Why were there never girls in cars with dragons in any of Auntie Kim's fables?

Could you still call them fables if they were real?

Andi opened a desk drawer, shoving a few pairs of glasses in multiple sizes and colors over and tossed the envelope of cash alongside them. Then she carefully stripped far away from her bed. She was guessing that the blue stuff wasn't poisonous, especially seeing as Damian had had so much on him, but she had no idea what it'd do to her washing machine. She should have asked him what was more appropriate—ritually burning her clothes or just throwing them in the trash.

But it didn't matter now because she could afford to buy new things—thanks to Damian.

She hadn't looked into the envelope, but she was sure it was full of hundreds—months' worth of scamming for overtime shifts for her, but nothing to him. Just money he'd found between his couch cushions; in his "castle" there were a lot of couches.

In the ordinariness of her room, his life seemed utterly impossible.

Andi went to rub her temple and caught herself in time. She desperately had to get clean.

For a slightly higher portion of the rent, she had the privilege of her own attached bathroom, and she went into it quickly, stepping into the tub and pulling the glass door closed. She turned the shower to maximum heat, knowing it'd take half of her shower for it to even warm up the way the pipes here worked. She went through half a bar of soap, lathering every part of her body, and then took her time scrubbing at her scalp and hair until she was sure it was clean. The entire time only one thought echoed in her exhausted mind: *what on earth could someone like him want with me?*

Is that what Mom thought when she first met Dad? Her mother had been a true romantic. She'd never met a Hallmark movie she didn't like, plus she'd been raised super sheltered. Which was why she'd fallen for all of their dad's lines—hook, line, and sinker. Even after she'd found out about the other family. *His real family.* Because it turned out she and Danny and her mom were the extra ones, which explained why he was mostly away on "business trips" when they were growing up. Her mother'd spent half their childhood covering for him, waiting for him to wise up and choose their family at long last, and it'd never happened. And once his other family figured out what he was up to, she'd made him give them up.

Andi would've liked to pretend that that part gave him pause—that he'd actually tried to fight for them—except she knew that wasn't true.

Mostly.

He did fight—but just for Danny.

Danny could carry on the family name. Seemed her dad's "real" wife had never given him a son. So, they offered Danny a place in the family; it would have meant skiing in Europe, summers in the Mediterranean, and fancy European boarding school like all the other super rich kids of Asia.

Danny'd torn up the letter on the spot, thrown it into the trash can, and spit after it—she could still see him doing that now in her mind, bright and clear—and it was the only reason she still put up with all of his bullshit.

Because he could've gone too, but he chose to stay.

Andi breathed in deep the steam of the shower and stepped on the tub's plug, sealing it up before turning the faucet on, catching all of the now hot water for her to soak in.

So, what did a dragon want with her?

When she'd woken in Damian's car, her first thought had been to escape, yes, when the wave of panic and memories of everything that'd happened hit. But she'd stopped herself. Why?

Because she knew if she got out, she'd be left with more questions than answers. And the longer she was with him, the more chances he might spill. She didn't have Auntie Kim to ask things of anymore, after all. And as she inspected her motivations, she found she really didn't want to go the rest of her life not knowing. It would be like going from the noontime sun back into a cave.

She sank down into the hot water up to her chin, thinking hard.

He'd been the first one to say "should" besides. To acknowledge that something more might even be possible—*somehow!*—between them.

And if she were totally, completely honest, it had nothing to do with curiosity, or him helping her out with the mess Danny had gotten her into.

It was *him*.

He was...extraordinary. In all senses of the word. And for some reason, he'd spent three hours watching her sleep when he could've been doing literally anything else.

Andi scrubbed at her face with her washcloth. Someone like Damian could buy and sell someone like her—with or without the dragon. So, it was stupid to think about him in any other context because rich assholes and disposable women was definitely a *thing*, and she'd sworn her whole life she'd never be like her mother. But then there'd been Joshua—the techbro who'd talked a good game for eight months before telling her she was "too much to handle"—conveniently dumping her right before his company's IPO, and now there was Damian.

So, what made Damian different? Was he different? Other than just the dragon?

Andi sank deeper into the tub, letting the heat soak in, remembering the way he'd looked at her in the pond. Intense, afraid for her, angry at himself—and unable to look away. Like he'd never seen anything like her before. More so after she'd saved his friend.

Andi wanted him to look at her like that again—like whatever she was doing was important; like the next words that she might say were precious; like he wasn't just seeing her but staring deep into her soul and understanding what he found there.

She could still remember all the places he'd touched her skin as the water in her tub lapped at her. The way he'd caught her wrist in the parking lot just now—afraid she'd leave angry at him. And when he'd picked her up and carried her into his castle, pressing her against his naked chest—if only she could've just clung to him in the pool instead. Even if she had been somehow bewitched earlier, would she really have regretted it if he hadn't stopped her in his bedroom? She remembered the way his hot hands had grabbed her underneath the fur coat, the way his tongue met hers with longing. She twisted to her side, pressing her cheek against the cold ceramic edge of the tub. Everything seemed so utterly impossible, but it didn't have to be.

All she had to do was text him.

Andi glanced at her phone through the glass shower door. It was on her bathroom counter. Ever since Danny had stood her up at the courthouse, she'd been carrying it with her everywhere like a little girl with a dolly—volume up, vibration on.

She rose, slid the door open, barely dried off her hands on a hand towel, and texted him, dripping wet: *Ten, tonight?* and then sat back down in the tub's warm embrace with her phone on the tile beside her. At least now, Eumie couldn't give her shit when they saw her next. She'd tried.

Which meant now she could hide back beneath the water because it was insane.

Oh, but only if he hadn't stopped her—if she'd twined herself around him in the pool when she'd had the chance. Looking back, it'd been totally unsafe, of course, but here in her tub, submerged under hot water with her fevered imaginings, she closed her eyes and ran her hands over her body, lifting her breasts out of the water and into the cooler air, tugging at her nipples. She remembered the way he'd pulled her to him, his hands so eager to take what they wanted—the way she'd been so ready to let him. She left one hand across her chest, making lazy circles around a breast as though it were a tongue while the other drifted lower...slowly. Was he the kind of man who would take his time and torture her thoroughly? Would he make her wait until she ached?

Or would he be upon her in an instant, irresistible and irreversible? Taking what he wanted, making her give herself to him?

She didn't rightly know, but the more she thought about him, the more she knew she needed to make herself come. She kicked the plug of the tub loose, setting the water to drain, then turned on the faucet again until it was as hot as he had been where he'd touched her, before laying back and sliding herself down until it was pouring between her thighs. All of her was slick and hot and finally clean, and if she closed her eyes, she could imagine him grabbing her hips to his, pulling her closer in time. She reached up and twisted the dial until the water was pounding, just like she hoped he would be, demanding and relentless, flowing over every part of her. She reached an arm back to push herself farther under its flow, arching her hips up, feeling the water pulse and surge—no mere man could ever hope to keep up with its intensity. But a dragon as a man, thrusting himself inside her... A dragon as a man, rubbing against her clit... A man—a dragon—just *might*—her toes pointed and her fists clenched and she had the wisdom to grab her washcloth and bite onto it before she screamed. She shuddered under the water as it licked her like a tongue until she was through with it and she could reach up to turn it off to lay panting in the tub, water seeping from between her thighs.

Samantha knocked on the wall through the hallway a few minutes later. "Everything all right in there?"

Her phone buzzed beside her. She pushed herself out of the tub to look down at the screen and saw his texted response: *Yes.*

She bit her lips, not sure if she was happy, scared, hopeful, or just a stomach-churning mixture of all three.

"Andi?" Sammy pressed, knocking on the wall again.

"I'm totally fine!" she lied.

CHAPTER THIRTEEN

Damian raced his sleek car through traffic, driving through the Briar's gates and up into the hills beyond. There was a certain path he'd run as a man so many times he knew it like the back of his hand. Whenever he'd felt the need to prove that this body was his and not his dragon's, it seemed the simplest way to feel that was to hurt it—running for miles on nearly desolate roads until he reached the final dead end, and even he was exhausted, covered in sweat, stopping at switchbacks and staring out at vistas few others got to see. It was in the course of those moments when he was punishing himself for existing that he often found clarity and maybe driving it now would help him find it again.

Andi hadn't run away from him—or from anything. In fact, she'd gone and put herself into even more danger. Why? Because it was the right thing to do, yes, but wasn't there a faint chance that she'd done it for him? To be—to stay—with him?

He'd had scads of women throw themselves at him before. He knew he was good-looking; he wasn't an idiot. He was handsome enough to have had an easy time with them without his money. But most women were blinded by either his presence or his bank account. He'd had precious few ever try to learn more about the man inside—nor could he afford to share—given what he was, what he did.

Which was what made Andi exceptional. Without trying to, and without any ulterior motive, she'd managed to see his reality.

And she hadn't run away.

She'd been scared—he'd read it in her eyes—but she'd stayed.

And she'd even fought to keep those memories! Which was only fair, considering the ones he now had of her. His car careened around another corner, almost feeling like he was in flight, the coin hanging under his rear-view mirror swaying as he imagined her swimming in the pool. The way her dark hair trailed out over the surface of his dragon's bathing pond, the way the water beaded on her skin as she emerged. The way she'd clearly wanted to mount him in his bedroom. How perfect her breasts were, both in the pond and when he'd gotten to touch one underneath the fur, remembering the weight of it in his palm, the quick tautness of her nipple at his touch.

Damian wanted to touch her, and he wanted to give her so much more. His hands wrung the steering wheel as he took another turn at high speed, feeling the pressure of his inseam against his now erect cock. The last of the succubus's poison working itself out? Doubtful. No—this was all him. Set on her. Set on being with her—being inside her. The thought made him rock-hard and stirred his sleeping dragon.

When would he see her again? She would text him. He was sure of it. Wasn't he? He craved her—he needed her—she *had* to text him.

And he knew he would ache until she did. Damian growled at himself. There were times when self-control was necessary, but now wasn't one of them. He had to take the edge off. He took another turn at breakneck speed and stepped on the gas as he reached for his belt, unlatching it quickly, before sinking his hand.

If he had followed her up the stairs to her apartment...if he'd caught her inside the door and pressed her against the wall...if he'd fit his mouth to hers and pushed his tongue in—he stroked himself rhythmically, in time to his thoughts, following the road from memory, increasing in speed. His cock in her mouth, then her hot thighs parting, him buried deep inside, thrusting, listening to her moan—he knew he was running out of road, but he felt like not coming was more likely to kill him than any accident. He needed this prelude—to exorcise his lust, to make it possible to just be himself around her the same way he wanted her to be around him.

Go take her, his dragon whispered.

Damian grit his teeth, still stroking. If his dragon had his way, they'd abandon the car now, fly back to her apartment, rip off its roof, and steal her away. The closer he got, the more willing he was to entertain doing it. He raced through another turn, his eyes half-lidded, and his jaw dropped, driving on instinct as he pumped his hand. In his mind, he was thrusting himself inside her, feeling her entire body tense…

Claim her.

Andi below him, calling his name, hips bucking…

Mate her.

In his mind, she came below him, and he reveled in the glory of it before letting it bring…him… home. He gasped—shuddering, momentarily transported—before he looked over the steering wheel and saw the road about to end. His foot slammed on the brake, and he yanked the emergency brake and the car spun in a squealing circle until it stopped, and he got out, angrily tucking his shirt back in—ignoring the warm, wet spot spreading against his stomach.

There was only a hair's breadth of space between the far side of his car and the guardrail. It would take a twenty-point turn to get him away from it without scratching anything. He stood at the end of the road and looked over it, at how close he'd come to needing to shift to save his life.

Andi, his dragon purred—perhaps the first time his dragon had ever used another human's name. *Mine,* his dragon said, and set him aflame with desire from the inside out. Damian staggered and caught himself on the car hood, cursing, trying to push his urges down. Instead of finding closure with his hand, he'd only opened Pandora's Box—and found his own dragon waiting inside.

How could he let himself get like this—over a human?

He reached for his phone and found a text waiting from her: *Ten, tonight?* and a slow liquid-like sensation of satisfaction perfused his entire body.

Yes, he typed back without hesitating.

CHAPTER
FOURTEEN

Andi woke up just in time to call in sick without getting into trouble, which was good because trouble was already waiting for her outside.

"This doesn't have anything to do with Danny, does it?"

She could hear Sammy interrogating someone in their living room—and could sense from Sammy's tone that her roommate's arms were crossed. Andi groaned and stretched in bed. She'd taken some ibuprofen before she'd gone to sleep, but she was the kind of sore that only moving more would fix.

Why? Because she'd taken a three-hour nap in a sports car that morning.

"Are you sure? Because Danny is bad news, and we don't want any of that around here."

She sat up in bed, blinking awake and listening. Sammy was talking louder now—on purpose. To warn her.

"Don't make me call the cops."

Andi's eyes widened. For Sammy to threaten that... She reached under her bed for her aluminum baseball bat. In a T-shirt and boxer shorts, she crept out to the living room, hugging one wall with the bat low. The hall was too narrow for her to take a proper swing, but she could take a decent golf stroke into someone's balls if she had to.

"Like I told you, she's asleep. I'll pass your message along."

"And like I told you, I'd rather wait." Andi heard the other person for the first time and realized it was a woman. A ball-shot was off the table, but maybe a crotch-shot would do. She peeked out of the hallway and saw Sammy talking to someone with platinum blonde hair. "There she is," the woman sitting on their couch said, turning. "Good morning, Miss Andrea."

The only one who called her Andrea anymore now that her mom had passed was... "Who are you?" Andi stepped into the living room and swung the bat up to her shoulder.

She turned herself on the couch to face Andi. She was dressed in a short black dress that made the stark-whiteness of her face and limbs brighter, and the deep red of her lips more menacing. The only thing out of place on her was what looked like a tiger-claw on the end of a leather thong around her neck, tucked against her cleavage. She stood, her heels making her tower over Andi. "Your esteemed uncle sent me. He has recently returned to town and desires to have dinner with you this evening."

Uncle Lee. She *knew* it. Andi groaned. "I'm going to work. I work nightshift. He knows that."

"So?"

Nobody else needed to know she had other plans for the evening. "So...I don't go out on school nights, Miss..."

"Elsa."

"Thanks, Elsa. I'm sorry he sent you for me, but we'll have to reschedule."

Elsa paused, then redoubled. "It will just be a light dinner; you'll be done well before your shift starts—"

"No," Andi said.

"Yes," the woman demanded, as though that made it so. Andi just stared at the woman, wondering at the gall of her, and Sammy started apologizing.

"She barged in here, Andi...I'm sorry...I'll get my phone—"

Andi waved her aside. It wasn't Sammy's fault; her uncle'd been trying to micromanage her life for as long as she could remember—him and all his money. She didn't think he meant to lord it over their poorer mother's side on purpose; it was just how he was. Only unlike their absentee father, none of his gifts ever came without a price. It was why she still had student loans. She couldn't stand the thought of him taking credit for her education until the day she died. Although she had contacted him when Danny'd run out on his hearing—because if her derelict brother ever did come back, he would need an amazingly expensive lawyer to stay out of prison.

But Danny's problems were his problems. And she wasn't going to give up her evening with Damian now—with no warning—at her uncle's say-so. Andi set the baseball bat down on the back of the couch. "Look, lady, I don't think you're going to wrangle me out of here in spike heels."

A smile fluttered across the woman's face. "You'd be surprised."

Andi snorted. She couldn't imagine her uncle dating someone quite so...blonde. But she could imagine him being thrilled to boss someone like Elsa around. She squinted. "Are you his secretary?"

"Akin to one, yes."

That explained it. If her uncle had told someone he'd hired to retrieve her, maybe they were afraid of getting fired if they failed him. Uncle Lee could also be a little bit of an asshole.

Andi held her hands out in a sympathetic fashion. "Okay...so, I've been dealing with him my whole life. And I know the whole impossibly bossy thing he does—he swans into town and then we're all supposed to drop everything and go see him because he's our uncle and who doesn't like red envelopes?" Andi couldn't remember how many Christmases and Lunar New Years Uncle Lee had saved just by showing up. "And I know he's my family...and I do want to see him! But tonight is just not going to be that night, okay? I don't know what he told you, but I'm sure he made me hanging out with him sound more important to your job than it really is. He's not going to fire you if I don't come back—swear. That's just how he talks; I promise."

Elsa frowned deeply. "Your uncle is the kind of man who gets what he wants."

"Yeah, I know." Andi pinched the bridge of her nose. "But right now, what I want is to heat and eat a frozen pizza and then go back to bed for a nap before work."

Elsa considered this. "All right. When can we reschedule?"

Andi sighed. *How about never?* But if there was anything her mother'd beaten into her thick skull, it was the importance of honoring her elders. And with Danny on the lam, her uncle—as distasteful as his obsession with being worshipped was—was all she had left.

"Next weekend. I'm off." That way she'd have time to brace for it. She'd listen to Uncle Lee talk about how important he was without ever explaining exactly why or how and tolerate him implying that she and Danny were ungrateful—both separately and together. She loved Uncle Lee; she'd known him her whole life, but he always acted like she was her brother's keeper—which she disliked—plus, it felt weird to reach out to him when she never knew what time zone he was in. The last time she'd called instead of texted had been when her mom was sick, and he'd been asleep in Sri Lanka.

He had still picked up though—and he was practically family. So, next weekend she'd tell him more about the latest stupid thing that Danny had done, and he'd feel an even bigger man then because Danny—once he resurfaced—really would need his help. She could see it on his face now like a movie marquee—Uncle Lee riding in one last time to help the Ngo twins out.

It really was a shame Danny wasn't around; first, because this was all his fault, and second, because he'd practiced enough to do a really stunning impression of their uncle.

Elsa typed very quickly on her phone, waited for a response, then returned her attention to Andi. "Very well. Your ride will be here next Saturday at seven o'clock. Try to dress appropriately for the occasion." The woman gestured to herself as an example, and Andi resolved to wear fuzzy pajamas with feet.

"Sure," Andi said. The woman stood, and Andi walked behind her, opening the door and seeing her out. She watched her gracefully take the flight of stairs and step into a car opened by a dapper driver wearing sunglasses even though it was dark out. But he wasn't as dapper as Damian had been. Andi bit her lips not to smile.

When she returned, Sammy was holding a pint of ice cream.

"Man, what a bitch. I should've just called the cops to teach her a lesson." Sammy dug into the pint with a spoon.

"What is this I'm hearing? Samantha O'Connor, admitting that sometimes the cops have a point?"

Sammy pointed at herself with the spoon. "I'm straight now, ain't I?" she said in her Irish lilt, her curly red hair in a tangled bun atop her head. She worked at a mom and pop body shop now—entirely legit—a complete one-eighty from the underground and illegitimate one she'd worked at when she'd been dating Danny, helping him fence stolen parts. Dating Sammy had been the best thing her brother had ever done, and dumping him had been the best thing possible for Samantha.

Andi grinned at her roomie. "You are. And...she's not worth it." Andi sank down beside her on their couch. This wasn't the kind of neighborhood where it was okay to call the cops—everyone here had a slightly guilty conscience due to one or more illegal side-gigs. Cops would make too many of their neighbors nervous, not to mention their landlord, if he learned of it. And cops in this town were the shoot-first-ask-questions-later type; she'd seen enough trauma cases at the hospital to know.

"I just didn't think anyone dressed in so much designer-shit would be that rude," Sammy said, shoveling a wedge of triple-chocolate fudge in.

Andi snorted. "The designer-shit makes them ruder."

"Pro-bab-ly," Sammy said around her bite, panting to not get a cold rush. "So how was last night? Everything you dreamed and more?"

Andi felt herself flushing. "I got paid well?"

"Cheers to that," Sammy said, tilting the pint up at her. "I was getting worried when you didn't come home in the morning."

"Oh, no, it was a twelve-hour thing," Andi said, covering quickly. "I didn't know until I was there, though. I spent all night watching someone's sick great aunt."

"Easy money then, too!" Sammy proffered the pint out to Andi. "Is it ice cream for breakfast or dinner for you?"

On a normal day off, Andi would've totally joined her, and they'd have booted Netflix up for the latest serial killer documentary. But while she'd already called in sick, tonight would be anything but normal. "Ummmmmm," she hedged, glancing at her phone.

In an instant, she had Sammy's full attention. "You're ditching me, aren't you? And not just for work." Sammy put her ice cream down and leaned over. "Why? Or rather...who?"

Andi fought not to flush. "It's...I met...it's not even a date."

"Um, yeah, 'cause it's after eight, and you're not ready yet—so it must be later—and later's edging into booty-call territory." Andi snickered, and Sammy went on the defensive. "What?"

"Say booty-call again." Andi tried to say it like she did, booty with an emphasis on the boooo.

"Don't think that making fun of my accent will get you out of telling me the truth, missy."

"Then don't be like that," Andi said, sticking out her tongue.

"So, who is he?"

"A friend."

"How'd you meet him?"

"Online," Andi said—and she wasn't even lying. She'd answered a Help Wanted ad after all.

"Oh, no, I never have time to date anyone," Sammy said, doing a halfway decent impression of Andi, before squinting at her. "Okay, then, what's your safe word?"

"What?" Andi's voice rose impossibly high, remembering the green room full of exotic black leather furniture she'd run through on the way to the pond inside Damian's castle.

"For when I call you later. To make sure you're not going out with a serial killer."

"Sammy, you watch too much TV," Andi chided.

"Um, no," Sammy snorted, then patted the empty space beside her on the couch. "Don't make me dust this couch cushion for Andi butt-prints." Andi laughed as she went on. "Besides, TV watching's just like masturbation and drinking. It's not bad for you if you're not doing it alone."

"I'm not sure about that, but okay, I give up," Andi said.

"Good, so what's it going to be? We should've set one up last night, too—I thought about it after you left." Sammy swept up her phone.

"Uh." Andi picked a word she never had reason to use. "Rambunctious."

"Okay. I'll call like twenty minutes in. If you start acting like I'm telling you there's an emergency, I'll play along, and if you say rambunctious, then I'll call in the troops."

Andi realized there would be no other way around this. "Fine," she said, and rolled her eyes affectionately at the other woman, before walking back down the hall.

"Hey, wait!" Sammy shouted after her.

"Hey, what?" Andi shouted back.

Sammy apparently twisted on the couch and sat on the armrest, leaning out so that she could waggle her spoon at Andi. "If you get laid, I want details!"

Andi waved her away and ran back into her room to hide.

WHAT DID one wear when you were meeting a man-slash-dragon whose shoes cost more than your five nicest outfits combined? And where were they going tonight? She'd only seen him in suits and dress shirts—and without any clothes at all—but she'd feel awfully silly if she dressed up and he arrived in jeans. She ripped through half her closet in a fit of indecisiveness and wished that she could call in Sammy for a consult, but there was too much she couldn't—no, *shouldn't*—explain. She didn't want memory erasing to be on the table for her best friend too. She'd shared everything with Sammy ever since she had moved in, so no wonder this felt weird now, but this was the kind of secret that was also a burden. Sammy had enough on her plate. If Sammy would even believe her—which was a stretch too—because would Andi have believed her if their roles were reversed? Hell no. She'd have probably thought Sammy had spent too long inhaling gasoline fumes.

In the end, Andi decided on wearing black capri jeans, comfortable chunky heels, a form-fitting blue top that matched the streak in her hair, and a black sweater that tied at the waist. Cute, but not sexy, because sexy might be foolish.

And then the doorbell rang, and she heard a thump. She glanced at her phone—it was only nine—and she didn't think Damian would be early, but maybe Uncle Lee hadn't taken no for an answer?

"I'll get it!" she shouted and ran up the hallway to possibly head off another of her uncle's emissaries at the pass.

She reached the door before Sammy had even gotten up off the couch, and peeked out the peep hole. There was no one there. She opened the door carefully and found a delivered box waiting. Sammy was always ordering car parts off of eBay...

"Sammy..." she began, pulling the box inside, but then found that it was addressed to her.

"What?" Sammy asked.

"Never mind. I forgot I ordered something the other day," Andi said, walking quickly back to her room.

"Cute outfit!" Sammy hollered after her.

"Thanks!" Andi shouted back before closing the door.

There was no return address on the box, and the label was typed —no handwriting. But precious few people knew where she lived.

She shook it, and when she didn't hear anything thump inside, she opened it. Inside, under a layer of deep purple tissue paper, was a sleek black silk dress so soft it kept trying to slip out of her hands. It had spaghetti straps and it was bias cut so that one of her legs would show more if she put it on—it was the definition of sexy.

Was this Damian's hint for his expectations about this evening? Or did he just want to make sure she didn't embarrass him when they went someplace nice? She wanted to be angry at him for assuming, but as she slid the dress over her head and it fell around her perfectly, she found she couldn't stay pissed. It was just that lovely.

She spent the rest of the time putting on makeup and doing her hair—running an iron through it so that it's straightness would be even straighter; deciding between strappy black heels and gold heels —and picking silver flats instead—because most of her nice jewelry was silver. At 9:58, she went back into the living room.

Sammy's eyes bugged out of her head as she clutched her heart in mock disbelief, and then she started dramatically rummaging through her purse.

"What?" Andi asked her.

"I'm pulling out my rosary to start praying for you. Forget serial killers. With a dress like that on, you're definitely going to murder a man."

"Sammy!" Andi laughed.

Sammy put her purse down and laughed with her. "No, seriously, why the outfit change?"

Because the guy I'm seeing wanted to see me in this? seemed a bit too strange to share. "I just felt like stepping it up a bit."

"And when'd you get that dress?"

She'd forgotten that Sammy had already seen everything in her closet. "A while ago," Andi lied—and the doorbell rang just in time to save her from any more awkward questions. Sammy gave her a smug look but stayed on the couch, and Andi could feel her roommate's future snarky comments percolating.

With a sigh, Andi opened the door, there was Damian. He looked like he always did—competent and strong—but he was dressed rather...normally. Jeans and a T-shirt and a snug fitting leather jacket. He was still hot, but they were definitely dressed for different places, and at seeing her, he gasped.

"You look amazing."

Between his expression of surprise, and the fact that he wasn't taking credit for it, she could've hit herself. The dress was clearly from Uncle Lee's henchwoman, meant for her to wear next weekend.

"Oh, God," Andi said, backpedaling into the living room while turning red. "I totally misread things. I'll go change—"

"No," he said and caught her wrist before she could disappear. "I would be an idiot to not want to be by your side tonight."

She slowed down, feeling the heat where his skin touched hers, flowing over and across her body like electricity. "Okay." Her black clutch was on the nearby table; she picked it up and turned to him. "I'm ready."

He let his eyes travel over her again, then smiled. "Let's go."

"Don't get too rambunctious!" Sammy shouted after her as she closed the door.

CHAPTER
FIFTEEN

Damian gallantly offered his arm to her as they walked down the metal staircase, past Eumie's now-closed Greek bakery downstairs, and she took it—just for the excuse to touch him again—feeling the bunch of his bicep underneath his leather coat. He opened the winged passenger door of his car—just as clean as the first time she'd seen it, somehow—and let her arrange herself inside before closing it gently and walking around to his own. By the time he'd gotten there, she'd slipped her shoes off and tucked her feet underneath her dress on the seat—her preferred mode of passengering.

He looked over at her before putting his car in drive. "So, did you think you had to dress up for me?" She could see him fighting not to grin.

"It's nice to see you again," she said, helplessly attempting redirection.

"It is nice to see you again, too," he agreed, showing more teeth by the moment. "But answer the question?"

"Fine." *The smug bastard. Might as well confess.* "Originally, no. But

I guess my uncle sent me this? For a meeting with him. It's just that I thought it was from you, and I think my head went all *Pretty Woman.*" *From a lifetime of hating rich people to being felled by a silk dress.* Andi rolled her eyes at herself.

Damian's eyebrows rose. "But I thought I couldn't buy you?"

"You can't. But that doesn't mean I don't like a new dress."

"I'll have to remember that," he said, giving her a wolfish grin before pulling onto the freeway.

DAMIAN DROVE just as fast as Danny had, but for some reason when he did she still felt safe. Maybe it was because she was sure none of the parts on his car were stolen. Andi snorted at the thought of her brother and watched the coin strung on a ribbon around Damian's rearview mirror sway every time he shifted gears.

"What's that?" she asked, reaching for the flickering gold.

"Careful," he said, without taking his eyes off the road. "It might give you scrofula."

Andi's hand paused, unsure if he was joking or not. "Okay, I'm a nurse, and even I'm not entirely sure what that is."

Damian chuckled, glancing over at her. "Me either. But the coin's a touchpiece. A thing that kings—who served by divine right in the Middle Ages—gave people with horrible diseases. The thought process was that if the king touched it, and the coin touched you, you'd be healed."

Andi batted at the coin like a cat, deciding to take her chances with old-timey cooties. "And why is it hanging in your car exactly?"

Damian made a thoughtful noise before answering her. "As a reminder."

"That you're a king?" she groaned, letting her disbelief color her voice. "Oh my God—"

"No, not anymore," Damian said, with an entirely straight face that Andi wasn't sure what to make of. "It was from a friend," he finished. "Who died."

"Oh." Andi bit her lips, feeling a little foolish now.

"It happens," he said, matter-of-factly, and she watched his jaw tighten while still staring at the road.

"No, yeah, I know," Andi said, swallowing a nervous apology.

"He thought it was funny because his name was Michael, and on the coin, it's St. Michael killing a dragon. A wyvern, if you want to get technical." Damian glanced over, this time at the coin, and she could see a rush of memories in his expression.

"How did he—" Andi began asking.

He cut her off, shaking his head and the memories away. "Maybe we could just not?"

"That's fine, I just..." she said awkwardly.

"I know," Damian agreed, nodding. "But...we're almost there," he said, pulling his car into an alley. Andi hopped out of the car before he could come around and get the door for her.

"I'm sorry," she apologized.

"Don't be," he said, gesturing her forward toward the restaurant's back door. The alley was full of trash cans, and the only light was a motion sensor that picked up as they approached, casting everything around them into sharp shadows. Andi walked up to the door, then turned back toward him, hesitating.

"Are you taking me to a murder factory?"

"If you're seafood, yes, but for humans, no." He leaned past her and rapped on the door with one hand. "I try to save murder factories for the third date." Her eyes widened, and he realized what he'd said. "Not that that's what this is, though."

"Oh, yeah, this is totally a coffee shop thing," she said, sweeping her dress up so that it didn't touch the ground.

THE DOOR BEFORE THEM OPENED, revealing a jolly man who took up most of the doorway.

"Bastian!" Damian announced.

"Little D! Come in, come in!" Bastian said, pulling back into the brightness of the kitchen, and Damian gave Andi room to follow him, as he made the rounds of waving or shaking all of the kitchen help's hands. It was like he was famous because—Andi realized belatedly—he was.

"Sorry about that," he whispered when he rejoined her in the hall.

"'Little D'?" she teased.

He leered at her, for half a hot second. "You tell me. You were with me in the pond."

She flushed red as Bastian bellowed, "Come in!" again, and they followed the sound of his voice.

They walked out of the kitchen into a hallway with polished cream-colored marble floors. Thick Corinthian columns stretched to a cavernous recessed ceiling lined with gently glowing hidden lights. The room was scattered with tables where other diners sat nearly done with their meals, sipping the last dregs of their wine and arguing over who would have the last bite of a shared dessert.

"This building used to be a bank," Bastian said, leading them down a short set of stairs. He pulled out a key, opened a door, and led them into a wine cellar. Andi was glad she still had her coat as they walked past rows of bottles, and then Bastian stopped in front of a very square door that had a lock just as esoteric as some of the ones she'd seen in Damian's mansion. "Just a second," he said, twisting a number on a dial, pulling on a bar, and then using a different key. A hissing sound began as compression engaged, and the obviously heavy metal door floated open—at least a foot thick—sliding out on a track on the ground under power. Its opening revealed a tastefully modern dining room and let the scent of lemon and wood smoke escape.

Damian walked in like he belonged there, but she hesitated, looking to Bastian. "What happens if you lose power?"

"Backup generator," Bastian said with a grin. "Although it's not really to make sure people can leave here. I'm working on homemade prosciutto—it's a two-year-long process. I'm not losing my refrigeration system unless there's a nuke."

Andi gave him a nervous smile and followed Damian, who was apparently holding her seat out for her—like that was a thing men still did—and she handed her coat over to Bastian, reluctantly.

"I'll turn on the heat," he promised, before leaving them.

Andi sat in the leather-cushioned chair as daintily as she could as Damian pushed it in for her. The room was narrow but long, and their table was only set for two, though it could've held twelve people easily.

"Where are we?" she asked, once Damian sat across from her, taking off his coat to sling it casually across the back of his chair.

"Belissima's," he said. A waiter swanned in out of nowhere and filled up one of their wineglasses each. "I thought the name was apt."

Very beautiful, she translated—and knew that he meant her. Oh, for the safety of her coat, now that she was sitting in sheer soft silk across from him.

"But...doesn't it take months to get reservations here?" she asked him. He looked imminently comfortable, like these leather seats were his second home.

"For some people," Damian said, swirling the wine in his glass. "Have you been here before?"

"No, but I've read about it." On multiple occasions. She might live under a rock, but her dreams were more worldly.

"It's better than what you've read. Trust me," he said, as half the kitchen staff came in through the still open vault door, setting down ten dishes all at once. "I know ordering for you is patriarchal bullshit, so I figured I'd order one of everything so that you could pick and choose, and we could be private." He tapped the table, and the waiter deposited the wine bottle they'd been hovering with before disappearing and closing the vault door behind himself, leaving them alone.

Andi gawked at their surroundings, the apparently locked door, and then at Damian. "You do realize this is faintly ridiculous."

"Entirely," he said with a predatory smile. "Eat up."

Seeing as she hadn't eaten since sometime yesterday, she was starving, and when it came to eating, her family was never shy. She had to at least try a little of everything—pasta, steak, wine, crab—because when would she ever get to come back? So, she collected a small mountain of food on her plate and then realized Damian was only eating steak just this side of raw. She took a few bites and worked up the courage to ask him, "So, like, when you eat, are you eating for two?"

He paused mid-knife cut. "Is that really the first thing you're going to ask me?" His tone was sharp, but his eyes said he was teasing, so she doubled-down.

"Runner-up was going to be if you hatched from an egg."

At that, he laughed hard, and she realized that might've been the first time she'd heard him truly laugh—ever—and in that moment, he sounded so free. She wanted to hear him laugh again.

"Answer the question?" she pressed, doing her best not to laugh back and failing.

"I had a mother. If I was hatched, I don't really remember it. I'm fairly certain she would have mentioned it to me, though. Your turn... how long have you been a nurse?"

She tilted her head, giving him what she hoped was a sarcastic look. "Didn't your background check tell you that?"

He waved her concerns away. "Shhh, I'm trying to seem less intimidating."

"Okay, then...four very long years.

"Always nightshift?"

"Pay's better. Slightly." She took a bite of lobster that'd been swimming in herbs and butter. He wasn't lying—the food was divine. But it was weird to be eating in a restaurant and have it be just them. She looked around at the space, and at the vault's closed door. Her, him, here—it didn't feel right. Then again, she had no idea what going out on a theoretical date with a dragon-man—or man-dragon?—ought to be like.

"What're you thinking?" he asked her.

"Will you walk into my parlor?" she quipped honestly.

Damian snorted and took a sip of wine. "I'm a dragon, not a spider."

"I notice you're not saying I'm not a fly." She tilted her head at him again.

His gaze swept over her as though inspecting her for himself. "You're definitely not a fly."

She fought not to flush under his attention. "I bet you say that to all the girls you bring here. Or...lady dragons?"

He set his wineglass down and considered her. "You might be surprised to find out that there are very few people like me."

"That must be so rough for you," she began, like she meant it, and then impishly added, "to have even a shred of competition."

He grinned at her, eyes glittering. "Oh, and just who is my competition, Andi?"

"I don't know. How thorough was your background check? I mean...did it list the three doctors I'm sleeping with?"

There was the smallest flicker of movement in his jaw as his teeth clenched, although nothing else in his smug, confident, smoldering expression changed—and she knew she had him. She covered her face with her hands and began cackling. "Oh my God, you actually thought I would date a doctor!"

His golden eyes widened in confusion. "Why not?"

"Says someone who has never worked with a doctor in their life," Andi snickered, and she shook her head at him. He only *thought* he had the upper hand. "So...have you always lived here?"

He made a thoughtful sound before answering her. "Mmm...here like on this mortal plane or here in this particular incidence of time and space?"

Was he finally going to tell her the truth? "Remember, I'm a nurse, not a physicist," she said, leaning forward.

He grunted and rearranged a series of smaller bowls on the table. "Let's say this is Earth, eh?" he suggested, centering his steak on the plate. "This, here, is another Realm, and this is another, and this is another." He went on, setting the roll plate, the butter dish, and a demitasse plate adjacent to 'Earth,' around them. "Most Realms, like most other planets, are useless—except for some travel considerations—but certain ones contain alternative forms of life and run off of non-scientific principles."

"Dragons...and magic?" she guessed.

"Your words, not mine," he said, still coy.

She squinted at him. "Then what happened the other night?"

"My people and I watch out for gates." He took a fingertip and stroked some of the blood from his plate out over its edge and onto the butter dish. "Gates let things that shouldn't be here, through. They're like rifts between different Realms." He touched the butter, then streaked it back onto his plate, before licking his finger.

How much was safe to tell her? It was the first time Damian had ever tried explaining the gates to a normal human aloud. He couldn't help but be aware of how crazy it sounded—no matter that it was accurate.

But just this afternoon, Jamison had managed to predict one of the smaller ones. He and Mills had rushed out to a rural grocery store while Damian'd been sleeping, and they'd sealed it off just as it started to leech Unearthly matter through. No one had been the wiser, although they'd bought the entire contents of the soda aisle just in case any of it had become contaminated—and Damian had a suspicion that even that was just because Jamison really, really liked Dr. Pepper. It was the first success they'd ever had on that front, and he hoped the first of many.

If he had met Andi in a few weeks—or a few months—would they even be having this conversation?

"So," she asked, pointing to his steak and butter in turns, "what are you?"

He settled back into his chair and observed her. How best to answer? It was hard to keep his defenses up when she was in that dress. The silk hung off of her in all the right ways, suspended by skinny straps he longed to reach over and break. He hadn't expected to open the door to a dream made flesh tonight, but he had.

His dragon roused. *She still smells good.*

Shush.

"What do you think I am?" he asked her.

He watched her gasp for air while thinking, and then stir the food on her plate. "Well, I don't think you're a vegetable," she said, pushing out a piece of broccoli. "And you're not a mineral," she said, dashing the table with salt. "So, you must be an animal. But there's a lot of different types." She pointed to beef, chicken, and crab in quick succession. "And I don't see Godzilla here on the table, sooooo..."

Was he just an exotic animal to her? He'd never considered that he might be. "Yes. So few places serve authentic nuclear reactor lizard these days, it's a shame," he said, snarking to cover up the flush of shame he felt. "Any other questions?"

"How long have you been doing this?"

And all of a sudden, she'd disarmed him again. He paused to think. There was the true-truth answer of twenty years, and then the just-truth enough. "Too long."

"Do you enjoy it?"

Such a good question, after so many dark nights. He took a longer sip of wine, considering. "There are...aspects of it that I enjoy. But it has its downsides. Like most jobs, I suppose."

"Why do you do it?"

Her tone was so earnest, he blinked. It'd been an eternity since he'd ever considered other options—and as far as he knew, they didn't exist. "Because someone has to. And I'm the best suited for the job."

Her lips twisted to one side. "Because of your thick skin?"

"Something like that, yes."

She sank back, looking at him. She'd been so intense, and now she was frustrated. "You still haven't told me anything I can Google."

Which was true, but it was for her own good. She had to know that, didn't she?

She needs to eat, his dragon murmured. Damian hadn't even realized his dragon was still paying attention. It was right. She'd stopped eating three questions in, and an entire table full of the most exquisite and expensive food in the entire city was growing cold as she tried to pump answers from him, and what was worse was, there was no way for him to not disappoint her. "Andi...it's not my fault that most humans don't think I'm real."

Her perfect lips pursed as her gentle brow furrowed. "But I do."

Andi's answer echoed in the room around them as he swallowed, feeling his carefully collected armor start to crack. Like scales sliding over scales, he felt a rearrangement of the space he held—as a man and a dragon—making room for possibility. He had known hunger, and he had known lust, but now what he wanted was something more, and he wished the table were narrower so he could reach across it and catch her hands with his, as she went on.

"And that's why I deserve the truth from you," she went on. "You're not normal—and I know that. So, don't lie to me, and don't pretend. I may not need to know everything, but I don't have time in my life for someone who holds back. I've had too many of those relationships before—they're not healthy."

The pain of something that hadn't shown up in his background check clearly arced across her face. "And what if I'm holding back for your own well-being?" he asked her.

Her full lips fell into a pout. He'd already noticed how often she would bite them when she was nervous—little did she know how that tempted him to bite them too. "Remember what you said earlier about patriarchal bullshit?"

Damian was forced to laugh. "Andi—" he began, ready to defend himself, which was becoming harder and harder in her presence, and then her phone rang. She blanched, and then reached for her clutch quickly.

"I'm so sorry," she said.

"Don't be. Take your time," he said graciously. He rather liked it when she was disconcerted.

"So, not now..." Andi said, instead of answering the phone.

"Are you rambunctious?" blurted out the person on the far end of the line, and Damian would've had no problem hearing them even as a human. Her next sentence was a little softer, though. "He was hot, so I gave him an extra thirty minutes to murder you, if you know what I mean."

"Thanks, and I'm fine," Andi said definitively, hanging up her phone and setting it far away from herself on the table before returning her attention to him. "My roommate was worried you were a serial killer."

"Well, she isn't wrong," he said. "To be worried, that is," he added, when her eyes widened.

"I guess that makes sense—considering what I saw." She stared at the table, likely remembering his dragon and the shimmer-tiger.

"It was fairly intense, and you were up close," he pressed. "All that blood and fear." If she was going to break, he wanted it to happen now, when he could escape with only paying in money.

She seemed to consider things for a long while and then looked up at him again, her gaze steady. "You'd be surprised how used to danger I am."

His dragon had heard the challenge in her voice and longed to answer. *Leave this place. Go and take her.*

Damian let his eyes trail over her, remembering the heat of her lips, the smooth sweep of her skin. She had to know what she was asking, didn't she? He could feel his urges, filling him up, making him ache. It felt like he'd done nothing but ache since he'd met her. And he knew if given half the chance... *No*, he told his dragon, feeling it roil in anguish before he finished his thought. *I'll take her here.* His dragon purred and settled in, waiting just underneath his skin.

"Is that so?" Damian asked aloud, staring across the table at her, waiting for her to back down or take back her words.

She raised her chin in defiance. "It is," she said with certainty. He grinned, and stood and grabbed the table between them, sending it spinning to the side, revealing her sitting in her chair. Glasses crashed, the wine bottle toppled, its red liquid pouring out, and dishes careened to the floor.

"Damian!" she gasped, clutching her napkin to herself like she'd just been exposed.

"How dangerous was that?" he asked, advancing on her. "On a scale from one to ten?"

Her eyes were wild. "I...I don't know..."

He lowered himself to kneel on his heels in front of her. "I thought you were used to dangerous things?"

"Are you trying to frighten me?" She frowned, looking down at him.

"If I am, is it working?" he asked while circling each of her ankles with a hand.

She gasped at his touch, and he could see her blood pulsing at her throat and breast, read the beating of her heart, and scent the smell of her sex—all before he started to slowly move his hands up. The only thing that could've made her more beautiful to him—if such a thing were even possible—would be if she were helplessly tied to the chair. She was panting now, small sharp breaths, and she whispered his name. "Damian."

"Yes?" he responded, like everything he had done and was doing was as normal as could be. Her skirt was up to her knees now, his hands barely higher. He kissed the side of her exposed inner thigh and felt her shiver.

She reached down and pushed a hand through his hair. "I think you should know," she began.

Oh Goddammit, this was going to be when she confesses that she's a virgin, and I'm going to have to rethink everything and go slow...

Her fingers curled in his hair and pulled him subtly in. "That on a scale from one to ten, this is only a two."

He looked up at her and laughed in delight before lightly biting her.

CHAPTER SIXTEEN

Andi knew she was not the type of girl that things like this happened to. Because above all else, Andi never—ever—lost control. She had to protect herself and other people at all times—like it was her job—because it *was* her job.

And yet, here she was, spread-eagle on a chair in front of Damian Blackwood with his mouth coming inexorably for her clit, and now that she was here, Andi realized, she wouldn't change a thing. She didn't know what would happen next, or how he was going to take her, only that he was—and that she wanted to let him. The loss of control—her inability to know quite what he'd do to her next—was strangely thrilling. She rose on her tiptoes, sliding shamelessly lower to expose more of herself to him as he took his time kissing up, up, up, until his hands reached underneath her dress to grab her ass and make her present herself at the edge of her chair for his mouth, pulling the fabric of her panties out of the way with his thumb.

Andi gasped as his lips found her, nuzzling against the light trim of her hair, bringing fingers up to spread her open so that he could kiss his way inside.

"Oh my God," she whispered as he kissed her hottest part. His lips were soft and teasing, brushing over her gently as she watched him, waiting with her heart in her throat until he opened them, and his tongue came out and pressed her *there* and made her gasp. His tongue stroked, his lips sucked, and suddenly every nerve in her body wanted to report in—like a wash of lightning over her skin—prickling up to her fingers and down to her toes. Her nipples felt hot like there was a direct current between them and his mouth, and the space between her legs where his chin ground in wanted more each time he kissed her. But *there...there...there...*his lips and tongue were so insistent and the sensation of electricity didn't stop. It only heightened. One of her hands curled on the chair's armrest, the other wound tight in his hair, and her hips ground up of their own accord. "What're you doing to me?" she whispered.

She'd meant the question rhetorically, but that didn't stop him from pulling himself away from her to answer. "I'm big. I want you ready," before rolling his tongue across her clit again and starting to push two fingers inside. Andi felt her body tighten and then give against him, letting him in.

"Yes," he purred, watching his fingers disappear inside her as she moaned.

"I hardly know you," she said, looking down at him. This truly was dangerous, even if she'd been the one to ask for it, even if she was loving every moment of it now.

"You know everything you need to," he said, watching her face as he pushed in and pulled out, like he was testing her, before slowly turning his hand palm up as he kissed her clit again. His fingertips started stroking deep inside her, making a come-hither motion, and she shuddered as they found the exact right spot. "I'm a man...I'm a dragon...and I want to make you fucking come." He whispered the words against her clit and then gave it a salacious lick. "Just...like that?" she breathed. "You think it's so easy?"

"You think I'm in a rush?" He chuckled into her; she could feel the rumble between her thighs.

It usually took her so long, unless she was just with herself, but there was something otherworldly about being here with him, and she gave herself completely over to the moment. She arched against his hand with a whine, and he purred again against her, following her with his mouth—his tongue sucking at her clit again before pulling back.

"I'm going to put another finger in you, okay?"

Andi nodded helplessly—anything to get his mouth back on her clit—and felt herself stretch as he pushed another finger deep inside. "Oh God..."

He instantly stopped pushing. "Oh God, yes, or oh God, no?"

"Yes," she whispered, bobbing her hips, begging for him to continue. He made a satisfied sound, as though pleasing her pleasured him, and started stroking her again, only this time while twisting his hand inside. Andi gasped. It'd been so long since she'd had sex, and Damian's hand made her feel so good and full and tight —and then his mouth found her clit again, and she arched back against the chair with a moan. She looked down, watching him watch her with his golden, glittering eyes, and reached down to run her hands through his straight black hair to pull his mouth tight to her. He growled, redoubling his efforts, speeding up his hand, running his tongue up her clit again and again as she felt everything start to tremble.

"Don't stop," she pleaded, putting one of her legs on his shoulder, opening even more of herself to him. "Just...whatever I do...don't stop..."

Whatever words he growled back were lost against her as her hips began to arch. His hand and tongue had wound her so tight so fast, and she was so...close...and ready to...let go...

Andi cried out, curling forward as her orgasm hit. Damian made a moan of satisfaction against her, burying his face between her legs, following her as she roiled, licking up every drop as his fingers fucked her through.

"Oh my God...oh my God," she breathed. Her body wracked with waves. His hands and mouth riding her, as all of her shuddered, her silk dress slippery against the leather dining chair, until she was just in the final twitches, suddenly aware of all the places that were slick from her, and all her exposed skin where she wasn't. She had just let this man—this dragon, take her—and she had come for him, around him, and small parts of her were coming still, and everything about her felt undone. "Oh my God," she said again, and finally meant it, realizing where she was and what had happened.

Damian rocked back and slowly pulled his fingers out of her, licking them clean before giving his mouth an aggressive swipe with his arm. "Did that rate above a two?" he asked, the corners of his lips quirking up.

Andi swallowed. "Definitely."

His smile became even more feral. "Then let me show you, say, a seven." And in an instant, he was on her, picking her up, carrying her to the wall behind her, kicking the chair she'd been sitting on aside.

His mouth met hers like he was starved the instant her back was against the wall. She could taste herself on him and feel the weight of his cock press against her as he pulled her hips toward his. He was like a freight train, and she had only moments to change course. She caught his face with her hands, holding him back, and he instantly stopped.

"There's no way anything bad can come of this, right? No eggs to hatch or STDs?"

He chuckled. She could feel it vibrating throughout his body. "No. Cross-breeding requires magical effort on both sides, and magic cures all ailments. I do have a condom though if it'd make you more comfortable—"

"No…but," she said, then quickly shook her head. "I'm on the pill."

Damian pulled back a fraction, to more easily meet her eyes. "What was the but about?"

It felt silly to admit, but this night was already on its own special —and strange—level already. Might as well go ahead. "I've never had sex with a guy without a condom before," she confessed.

He held still for a long moment in which she was afraid she'd said the wrong thing, then began clearly reaching for his wallet. "Then I can—" he started.

"It's okay." She grabbed his arm to stop him. "If you're sure about the other things, it's okay."

"You're sure you're sure?" he asked her earnestly.

She nodded and watched his eyes narrow in concern before asking, "You're not a virgin, are you?"

It was her turn to laugh. After everything he'd done to her. "Do you even have to ask?"

He grinned wickedly and rocked into her with intent—making her feel the way he wanted to fit her body—and she bit back a moan. "Different people count different things."

"Well, I guess I am a virgin then," she said breathily. He paused again and his eyebrows rose. "When it comes to fucking dragons."

He made a sound deep in his throat that didn't sound entirely human, that made her both shudder and shiver—and want more. "Not for long, you won't be." He reached up her skirt to pull her panties down, and his other hand went for his belt.

Her hands met his there, unbuckling his belt. As she kicked her underwear off, she helped him, shoving his jeans down, releasing him. Damian moaned as she touched him and watched the expression on her face as she took stock of him with a stroke. He hadn't been lying—he knew he was large—but he knew she was wet and ready. He leaned forward again, kissing her, feeling her perfect breasts through her thin dress and then reached down to grab one of her legs to pull it around him, sending the silk of her dress cascading back and down, so that nothing remained to block his path. He held her there, pressed against the wall, kissing her madly as he placed the head of his cock against her, nudging up. With her leg wound around his hip, she was open wide for him, and with a sigh of release, he started pushing his way inside.

"Damian," she whispered as he felt her stretch to take him in.

"I'll go slow," he promised and started rocking her into the wall.

With each small stroke, he felt the naked friction of skin against skin and relished it. Knowing that this was the first time Andi'd ever let someone take her without protection made him want to claim her possessively. Any man who wouldn't wear a condom was a cad, but any man who said he didn't feel a difference was a liar, and the thought of being the first man to get to come inside her made his cock throb. He bent over, kissing her hard, her mouth fitting perfectly to his, letting him feel each of her moans as he slowly slid in. So close to what he wanted and what was easiest to get it, he reached down and picked her up entirely, spreading her ass with his hands, to pull her hips to his so that her legs could lock around him at the perfect height, slowly settling himself in, in, in, close, close, close.

"Yes," he hissed, thrusting up, finally all the way inside, locking them together as she moaned. "Ever since you got into my car last night," he said, breathing into her neck, "I've wanted this."

"Wanted what?" she asked him breathily, looking up. For a sharp second, he worried she was making fun of him, but her eyes were glazed with sex, her long hair in sweaty tangles around them, and he knew that her mind was lost and her body had won. He was the one who was supposed to be half-animal, and yet here he'd completely reverted her to something primal. He smiled down at her wickedly, with an expression that in other circumstances had made men turn and run in fear, before nuzzling his mouth against her neck to whisper, "To eat you. To fuck you."

To claim you, his dragon chimed in.

His dragon was riding him so quietly he'd almost forgotten he was there. His dragon enjoyed sex as much as killing—he was always present when either was in the offing—but this time, it was as if the beast had been holding back.

Is that what you want? Damian asked it, sincerely.

Before his dragon could respond, Andi's hand was on his chin, pulling him to look at her, fully present again. "That's what I want too." Her eyes were sharp, and her ankles were locked behind him, trapping him to her.

"Which part?" he asked her, barely daring to breathe.

"The eating, the fucking. All of it." She squirmed against him, begging him with her body to continue. "Fucking fill me up."

Damian and his dragon growled with shared intent at the exact same time.

It was his turn to lose himself after that—to lose himself in her. He brought her hips to his, again and again, feeling her pussy slick him, stretch, and swell as she got close. He buried his face in her neck, her breasts, her hair, kissing whatever he could, tasting silk and salt in turns. He thudded his hips into hers over and over again, amazed each time at how she fit him perfectly—and he knew he'd never get enough. And then he felt the shift in her as she writhed against him—grinding herself on him as he fucked her, her panting moans and high-pitched whines—and he knew he was going to make her come again. Only this time while he was buried deep inside her, and he would get to feel her pussy squeeze his cock and not his hand. The thought of her coming around him somehow made him even harder, the need to take her fiercer, and it was like there was something flammable building up inside of him, waiting for her match to strike.

Her arms were wound around his shoulders, holding on for dear life, her head thrown back, her shameless cries bouncing with each of his thrusts, until the moment when she screamed, "Damian! Oh, Damian...oh my God..." and clawed his back through his shirt with her fingernails, and he knew, oh, he knew. He redoubled his thrusts, feeling her milk him, both wanting it to last forever while knowing that if he waited for another second he would die. He held onto her with one hand, pinned her against the wall with his hips, and punched the wall to the side of them to try to make it last and then...

"Yes, God! Yes!" he shouted, unable to hold himself back anymore, as a flurry of drywall dust scattered down. He spasmed into her, shoving his hips up, thrusting his coming cock deep inside. "Andi, Andi, Andi," he said, calling her name with each pulse of his cock, claiming her with his cum, making her take it, keeping himself inside her until he was sure he was utterly spent, and then taking a few more strokes after that just because she felt so fucking good.

He slowly let go of her, letting one of her legs sink and then the other so that she was standing shakily on her own two feet like a newborn colt and he had a hand on either side of her—as if he were holding up the wall. Her eyes met his, as her dress slipped down to cover her from him again. They were both slicked with sweat and breathing hard, and at that moment, he felt completely exposed to her—and completely human.

"Satisfied?" he asked her, the same as he had earlier in the day.

She gave him a sly smile, remembering her former answer, and breathily pushed a lock of hair out of her face. "Not even vaguely."

Be careful what you ask for, his dragon warned her—and his moment alone was gone.

Damian just shook his head and pushed himself away from the wall as he adjusted himself. That...had been spectacular. She was amazing. And there was so much more he wanted to do to her—and what's more, he felt she may be game. He closed his eyes, remembering the wanton way in which she'd already given herself over. He was half-tempted to command her to fall to her knees right now, just to see if she'd obey. To tie her hands behind her with her napkin and blindfold her with his and—*not here,* he told himself. *Not yet.* He took a deep and cleansing breath, willing his urges down, telling himself to be pleased with what he'd already gotten—no matter that all it did was make him hunger for more. When he felt in control again, he opened his eyes to the destruction all around them.

His dragon was unfazed, but he knew this was what happened when he was around. Broken glassware, spattered food, toppled chairs, the dent he'd made in the drywall—and in the fucking metal of the vault behind it—to distract himself from coming, just to extract a few more moments of sheer pleasure from her body.

Their dining room represented all the chaos and danger of being near him, especially when he let himself loose. The people who worked for him, they understood. But Andi – even when she'd taunted him and wanted him to press on—didn't know any better. She didn't know what she was asking for in the least.

He glanced over at her and caught her looking around the room herself, her eyes widened in surprise. *See?* he told himself.

He had no right to torment her with his presence, much less any of his desires. She was too beautiful, too smart, too funny—and too human. She didn't deserve this. He couldn't drag her down to his level.

Not even if she wanted to go with him willingly.

CHAPTER
SEVENTEEN

It took Andi a moment to parse all the destruction—after she'd found her underwear again and pulled them on. Between the table that Damian had shoved, the food on the floor, the wine they'd spilled, and the chair, and the wall—not even counting what he'd just done to her—she put her hand to her mouth. "Wow. That... was a lot."

By then, Damian had himself tucked away back inside his jeans, and he shrugged. "I can afford it."

"That sounds like something a villain might say." She glanced over at him as he turned toward her. Something in his mood had shifted, but she didn't know what.

"At any point in the last thirty minutes, did you want me to stop?" he asked.

She bit her lips before speaking. "Not really, no. But that doesn't mean I'm used to this...this...mess."

He inhaled, as if he were going to say something, then changed his mind and said something different instead. "That's what I'm good at. Making messes. And only sometimes cleaning them up." He righted the chair that he'd kicked, and then went for the table.

Andi watched him. There'd been a subtle change in his demeanor. She couldn't have pointed it out to a jury, but it was making her nurse-sense all tingly. It was the same feeling that you got in certain rooms when you knew you shouldn't turn your back on a patient—not because they were going to hit you, but because they were going to code.

"Life is always messy," she said softly.

He snorted, picking up the table to return it to its proper spot. "I imagine working in the hospital gives you certain skills, and for what it's worth, I don't enjoy the messier aspects of my occupation. But I'm not sure that that makes it any better philosophically when it keeps happening to me." He made sure to look her directly in the eyes when he spoke next. "Just because you are used to a thing doesn't make it safe or good."

She squinted at him. "If I didn't know better, I'd think you were trying to scare me off."

"Because I am," he admitted.

"By taking me out to the best restaurant in the city and then fucking my brains out?"

Damian chuckled darkly and gave her an indulgent smile. "Oh, Andi, I never said I was smart." He walked to the vault's door and hit a button on its side. Andi heard the muffled tones of a bell ring and watched him pull out his wallet as he returned. "So, how much should I pay you, princess?"

She froze. "Excuse me?" she said, trying to keep her voice flat as her heart beat up into her throat. Everything—from her last boyfriend, to shit with her uncle and her dad and Danny—all of it came rising up, and it took all of her strength to stay still and not let anything show.

"I'm cleaning up my messes. Surely your fancy dress needs cleaning too," Damian said matter-of-factly—like five minutes ago, he hadn't been calling out her name when she'd let him come inside her.

She flushed in deep shame. "Are you being a jerk now on

purpose?" He didn't deign to respond; he just started pulling out and folding a hundred-dollar bill lengthwise. "Has anyone told you that you're very good at it?" she questioned, blinking back tears while wanting to punch him.

"I'm showing my appreciation," he answered, as he leaned forward and slid the money underneath the strap of her dress with a practiced hand like it was a stripper's thong.

"I see," Andi said. She swallowed tightly. This was what happened when she trusted people—men, stupid rich men—even for a moment. She held a hand up as if to pardon herself and turned around looking for something—anything—and found it. A carafe half-full of water that had somehow survived their destruction. She picked it up, brought it back, and calmly threw its contents at his face.

He closed his eyes in time but let the water hit—he had to've known what she was going to do before she did it. He reached up afterward to flick wet hair out of his face as the rest of it soaked into his shirt, and he narrowed his golden eyes at her. "I suppose I deserved that."

"Go fuck yourself," Andi said, as her phone went off again. She went and retrieved it and her clutch from the floor, welcoming the interruption to…whatever was happening between them now.

"Hello. This is General…" began a robotic voice on the far end of the line. She turned her head away from Damian to concentrate. It was an automated message from her hospital, an all-hands-on-deck plea for any available staff to come in. The last time she'd gotten one of those was when a tanker turned over on the freeway and caused a twenty-car pile-up.

Just as she hung up, Damian's phone rang too. As he took the call and paced to the far wall of the room while listening, she removed the hundred-dollar bill and crumpled it up, dropping it to the floor.

"Are you all right?" he asked. And then, "I'm on my way." He hung up and looked over at her. "I can't take you home. I'll call a cab."

She wanted to ask why, but who was she kidding; there was no way he would tell her. "You really know how to treat a girl."

There was a flicker of pain in his expression—so fast that Andi wouldn't have noticed if she weren't so trained to look for it—and then he went entirely aloof. "There's trouble. You know what kind. I have to go." He was already putting on his coat.

She looked at the phone she held, and then over at his. "Does that trouble involve a certain friend staying at a certain place I work at?" He took too long to respond, so she knew it did. "Just drive me there."

"What?"

Andi shook her phone at him. "Work just called. They're offering double time, and there's still seven hours left tonight."

"I just gave you ten thousand dollars this morning."

"Some of that is spoken for, which you already know."

He sliced through the air with his hand. "No, I'm calling you a cab—"

"Which I'm going to tell to take me to work then." She picked up her clutch. "I've got spare scrubs in my locker, and I always bring my badge, for opportunities like this." She flashed him the inside of her wallet, where her badge was like a cop.

"You reek of sex."

"As do you, but I've got bath wipes in my locker because sometimes my job isn't sanitary. Besides, you have no claim nor say in what I do."

He growled and lunged back to the door to hit whatever buzzer he'd hit earlier.

"Sorry, sorry!" said Bastian, appearing on the other side of the opening vault door. Bastian blinked at the damage, then swallowed visibly. "Dessert? Nightcap?"

Anger ignited within Andi. This was apparently so normal, it wasn't even worth commenting upon. How many other women had Damian brought here and then wrecked the room with?

Andi put on her best smile, one honed by years of front-line customer service. "We're done here. Thank you, it was truly a meal to remember." And then she strode out into the hall. He could follow her or not.

"Add all of this to my tab," Damian said behind her, confirming her guess. How could she have been so stupid—to think somehow she was special? She heard him following her as he asked, "Where do you think you're going?"

Andi quickened her pace, darting through the empty restaurant, needing to put distance between him and her. "Like I said, to work."

He grabbed her arm just inside the back door of the kitchen. She tried to shake her arm free, but he wouldn't let go. "Put your coat on," he commanded.

She gritted her teeth and turned on him, still trying to wrestle from his hold. "Let me guess, it's for my own good, and you're not going to tell me why?"

"We're in a rush," he said forcefully. "Put on your goddamned coat," he said in a tone that broached no argument.

Andi dug in her heels. She practically got paid to argue with people at work—she wasn't going to let herself be bullied now. "Why should I trust you? With anything at all?"

His eyes darkened, and he let her go, stepping back. "You're right. You shouldn't." It sounded like a confession to her.

Andi put on her coat for herself—*not him*—because it was cold out and her dress was thin. But after that, he reached for her, and though she couldn't say why, she didn't move away.

He popped her collar up, then opened the door.

And right outside, someone was waiting—with a camera and a flash. She squeaked when it went off, and Damian propelled her to the passenger side of his car, holding his own coat out to try to protect her, tossing it into his car after her. *So much for getting her own damn ride out of here.* The flash blinded her three more times before the door closed all the way and it was so disconcerting—she pushed her silk skirt down, hoping she hadn't accidentally flashed anyone, experiencing a sudden strange sympathy for celebrities.

Damian was cursing under his breath when he got in. He popped the car into reverse. He didn't look back first, although she heard photographers leaping out of the way. She guessed that when you were a billionaire, you could handle a manslaughter charge.

"Does that happen often?" she asked.

"No." He wheeled the car around so quickly it made her stomach twinge, and then landed in drive to take off. "Because I never go out."

She folded her arms. *Liar.*

"You don't believe me," he said.

"Why should it matter to you?"

He ran his fingers through his hair. "Look, the last few times I went to Bastian's wasn't with dates. It was with...trouble. We covered it up by leaking some crap about wild parties. The paparazzi know that billionaire bad boy exploits sell ads."

She twisted to look back the way they'd come. "How did you know?"

"It took too long for them to check in when I rang. They needed to give the photographers time. I doubt it was Bastian personally, but I'll put him on notice after this."

Andi kept her arms folded around her, deliberately not looking at him, but it was impossible to forget that he was there. She watched the coin swinging underneath his rearview mirror in silence, wondering if she'd made the right choice yesterday. If she'd let him make her forget everything that had happened, she'd have been at work tonight anyhow without any of the drama, mysteriously richer and dragon-free—and she never would've come like that, for him or around him. She felt her thighs getting warm at the memory, her body betraying her still very pissed off mind, and she squirmed.

"Can you turn off the fucking heated seats, please?"

Damian scanned his dashboard. "They're not on." Then he jerked his chin at her side of the car. "What'd the hospital tell you?"

"It's a robocall we get when they want us to come in," she said in a tone she hoped conveyed how little she wanted to exchange words with him. The sooner she got out of his car, the better.

All her life, Andi had just been an afterthought to her family. According to Auntie Kim, all her older relatives had rejoiced at her mother's pregnancy: twin sons, which meant double luck on the clan. Danny had come out just the way he was supposed to as the much-hoped-for boy, whereas she'd started life as a disappointment —because no girl could ever rightfully pass on the family name and legacy.

She dared a glance over at Damian and saw him in profile, watching the road intently. It was like she came with a fucking manual, and he'd read it somewhere—*maybe in her background check?* She snorted, then looked out the window again. *Go ahead and treat Andi Ngo like dirt. It's what she's used to. Don't even feel bad about it. No one else ever has.*

FOR THE FIRST time in a very, very long time, Damian did not know what to do.

In the restaurant with Andi, he'd just wanted to answer her challenge with his own, to prove to her that whatever she thought she could offer him he could take that and double it—and a dark part of him had wanted to ruin her for others, taking all of her for him.

But fucking her had been too perfect. She fit him like a glove, and he fit her like a key, and if he thought about it for too long now, he'd definitely get a hard-on again. *Goddamn.* Without ever having had it before, he knew they'd had the kind of sex that made men's heart's soft, with a pull so strong it could yank an arrow from its path.

But he was a *dragon*. And he had people to worry about—not to mention civilians. His life was not his own.

So, he'd hurt her. Like an asshole. Intentionally fulfilling every fear he thought would trigger her from her file. He'd watched his words wash over her and he'd known the whole time he'd said them just how bad they'd make her feel and now she was curled up like a comma in the car beside him.

His hair was still wet from the water she'd thrown at him, and he didn't blame her for that—not one bit. He dared a glance over at her and saw her staring out the window with a small frown. She was still beautiful, even when angry.

Especially when angry, his dragon said, and it was right.

Why was he so drawn to her? What magnetic north for him did she possess?

Why was hurting her like hurting himself?

Damian dared a second glance. She'd turned, so her hair hid half her face from him and he wanted to stroke it back, feel his fingers part it to expose her jaw and neck, and then take so much more. He ground his teeth together, refocusing on the road, trying to force wild parts of himself down. His lust was hard to conquer as his dragon. *Goddamn,* he thought again. Every inch of him still wanted her. He would be a fool not to after she'd made him feel like that—it would take weeks—if not years—to erase the memory of her from his body, and his Forgetting Fire did not work on him.

What was it about her that made him weak? He'd hurt hundreds of people in his lifetime—maybe thousands—and here he was, half-dragon, worried about what a single mortal human thought of him.

His hands wrung the steering wheel, and then he turned toward her. "Austin said Zach was in danger."

Her attention was on him again in an instant, and he knew she'd caught the fact he'd given her former patient a name. "What kind?" she asked quickly.

He downshifted, swept into the left lane of the highway, and then upshifted again. "The types of danger that my kind of people get into." He hit one hand against the steering wheel, angry at himself for breaking. "Look, I can't be holding your hand right now, Andi."

She took off her shoes and tucked her feet under her skirt on the seat again, making herself small, and he fucking felt bad—him! Bad! What was it about her?

You like prey that fights, his dragon told him.

Stay the fuck out of this, he told it back, and then looked at her again. "I'm not apologizing," he told himself more than her through gritted teeth.

"I'm not asking you to," she said primly, then rolled her eyes with a sigh. "Don't worry, I'm used to doctors."

And now she'd categorized him directly into the box he'd wanted her to at the restaurant. He was clearly like every other asshole in her life. Well, two could play that game. "It's not just you, you know. I'm like this to everyone," he muttered.

"Oh, hooray, then," she said with extreme sarcasm, as they took the next exit off the highway.

CHAPTER
EIGHTEEN

"Wait here," Damian told her the second the car was in park outside her hospital.

Was he ever going to get tired of bossing her around?

"Uh, no," Andi said, getting out ahead of him. "You think they're just going to let you in?" She stared at him over his car's roof.

"I have plenty of cash on hand."

Of course. He assumed that he could just buy anyone. Andi shuddered, almost physically repulsed. *What on earth had she ever seen in him?* "People at the fancy restaurant may know who you are, but security here doesn't. And they have a pension and they like their jobs. So, whatever you've got in your wallet isn't going to incline them to break the rules for you." She stepped out from around the car and started bunning up her hair. "I'm the only one with a badge, so if you want to get in, you're coming in with me. Or you can waste your time. The choice is yours." She turned and started walking toward the stairs, and after half a second, she heard him follow her.

She led him down the covered sidewalk to the hospital's door, where a security guard was waiting at a kiosk right inside, peering anxiously out into the night. She knocked on the door, watched him jump, and then saw him hit the switch to open it inside his kiosk.

"Everything okay, Omar?"

It took him a moment to place her. "Nurse Ngo? Look at you, all fancy!"

"Ha, thanks," she said, grinning at him. "They put out a robocall. Are we Code Black?"

He leaned forward so she could hear him better. "Getting there, sounds like. Shooting downtown. They haven't caught whoever did it yet." He rapped his knuckles against the glass protecting him. "The ICU's so busy, they stopped answering phone calls. Plus, it's a full moon, you know?"

Full moons at hospitals were legendary. While she didn't believe in superstitions, it was hard to not think they were true when every patient who was even remotely psychotic chose the night of the full moon to act up.

"Oh, man. Well...I'd better get to work, then." She grabbed Damian's arm. "This is my friend...he's dropping me off...just coming in to use the bathroom."

"Sure thing," Omar said. He hit the button for the next set of doors and waved them through.

DAMIAN WAITED until they were well down the hall before asking, "Code Black?"

"When the hospital's too overwhelmed to take any more patients—not enough staff or beds." She hit the button to summon an elevator. Zach had to be in the intensive care unit, which was her own floor. Hell, she might get assigned to him tonight.

"Then what happens?"

"We start diverting patients elsewhere. We're not the only hospital in town—just the biggest and best." An elevator appeared, and they both stepped in. It was hard not to feel trapped in an enclosed space with him. For some reason, it felt like he took up too much room—breathed too much air. Maybe it was the dragon she knew was inside him.

Damian's expression clouded. "Are you ever in danger here?"

She half-shrugged, waving away his fears. "People have brought guns in here before, yes. But we get amusing 'violence prevention!' classes once a year where they try to teach us jujitsu to break chokeholds."

"You're kidding," he said, glowering.

"Not in the least."

The elevator dinged, the doors opened, and he blocked her exit with an arm. "Okay. Thank you. Go home now."

"Now? You're kidding, right?" Andi took a step back and crossed her arms. It was time to set him straight; she'd suffered through too much nonsense already this evening. "I think you misunderstand our current relationship here, Mr. Blackwood. You're not my employer, not my family, not even a friend. You're just some brand-new fuck buddy with no say in what I do. And this?" she said, gesturing at the walls around them as the elevator started its 'stop blocking the door' alarm, "Is a hospital. Where I am a nurse. There are people here who *actually* need me, so if you don't mind—or even if you fucking do—I'm going to work."

She was darting down to pass under his arm when he swooped her up, pushing her against the back wall of the elevator before she even had time to gasp. And then when she tried to, it was too late. He silenced the sound between his lips as he leaned in—his whole body matching against hers.

Andi grabbed the collar of his coat to hold on as he kissed her, unsure if she was going to pull him in more or push him away. Heat thrilled through her, her whole traitorous body responding to him—as if at his command—and she fought not to let herself moan because his strange physical power over her was unfair. *She didn't need him, she was better than this, she shouldn't have to put up with*—but his hands were in her hair, and he kissed her like he needed her to live and while she didn't want to get hurt, she wanted to be wanted like that—and she wanted to let go and let herself feel that way too.

The elevator—which had given up on them—returned them to the first floor. As it opened, Damian took a step back and hit the right button again without looking, keeping his eyes on hers. "Just a fuck buddy, eh, princess?" he said with a smirk, his golden eyes full of fire, and it took the strength of every individual atom in her body to not sway as he released her.

"Yes," she whispered, not entirely in answer to his question but more as a response to what had happened, and as the elevator doors reopened on the right floor, she ran for them.

"Goddammit, Andi," he said, chasing behind her.

She kept running, trying to stay focused. How come he could make her feel like that? It absolutely wasn't fair. She quickly redid her hair bun, from where his hands had messed it. "I'm going to work. It will be utter chaos in there—people screaming and dying. This is a hospital, and I'm a nurse. This is what I do," she told herself more than him. She flipped her badge out to swipe it at the next set of doors and when they opened automatically it sounded like there was an entrance to hell distantly beyond.

"Well, you weren't wrong about the screaming part," Damian said and took the lead, running forward.

DAMIAN REALIZED he would have to shove Andi into a broom closet and then tear the handle off the door to get her to stay behind as she ran beside him, swiping them through the next set of doors with her badge. He couldn't lie, running toward battle with her by his side like some kind of humanitarian Valkyrie was hot as fuck, but he couldn't take the risk of anything happening to her.

Like we'd let it, his dragon muttered.

Michael? Zach? he reminded his dragon of their failures and felt its anger rise.

She is different!

But we're the same! Which was why he'd gone one-hundred-percent asshole at the restaurant and had maintained at least eighty-nine percent in the car ride here—until the elevator ride when she'd called him a fuck buddy. Something had changed in her scent when she said the word "fuck," a hint of arousal that he would have missed had he been human. But he wasn't. And the dragon within him would not allow such a ludicrous denial of the connection between them. Just a fuck buddy? No fucking way. He'd *had* to erase the words from her lips with his own.

But she wasn't wrong about anything else. He—and his dragon—were assholes, and he knew it. Another reason why he knew he was doing the right thing in pushing her away.

They burst through the final set of doors into what he assumed was her ward because she paused and put her hands to her lips and whispered, "Oh my God."

The screaming was louder, and the nearby furniture was in disarray—computers dashed to the floor—and there was blue streaked against one wall. People—staff and patients and visitors—were huddled inside of rooms with the curtains drawn for what good they would do, and some of those who had strength had barricaded their rooms with the visitor couches.

"Fuck," Damian hissed, and then whirled on her. "Where's the safest place here?"

"What?" she responded, blinking quickly.

"The safest place. I'm taking you there," he said, grabbing her shoulders. "Now!"

Andi snapped out of it, her stance firming. "No!" She glanced around at the chaos and looked at the lone monitor remaining, her eyes tracking something he couldn't see. "Room three," she said to herself and started running down the hall.

"Andi," he growled, chasing after her. She stopped to yank a red cart away from its wall, like the same one that Austin made Grimalkin conjure after Zach'd gotten hurt. He paused in front of it, blocking her path for a moment, as she shoved the cart at him. "Andi—"

"There's no time!" she shouted, angling the thing around him. "You do your job, and I'll do mine!"

"Goddammit, Andi," he cursed, and then he heard it—a sound that wasn't to human ears, at least—the low, keening subsonic frequency of a lurker, the kind like elephants used to call across the plains. He could only hear it because of the dragon in his blood. It was close, and it was the way Andi'd just run.

Damian hurtled down the hall after her, feeling his dragon course just under his skin.

Free me! it commanded, trying to take control.

No! he told it, shoving it down.

He rounded the corner and saw Andi running full bore with the cart, down to the second from the last room, where a nurse had dared to open the door and was directing her in with both arms like an air traffic controller—completely oblivious to the fact that a lurker was crawling across the ceiling above her as fast as it could.

"COME FIGHT ME!" he shouted at it, and as it paused, his senses heightened, and the world around him slowed. He was either going to get there in time or be scarred for the rest of his life by his failure—worse than losing Michael, worse than watching Zach get hurt. His dragon beat on him from the inside with hot fury and the only reason he didn't let it out was that he knew there was no time. He raced down the hall with superhuman speed, just as Andi reached the door.

"DON'T TURN AROUND!" he shouted at her, willing her to shove herself inside the room, as he leapt onto a sink counter and threw himself up to where the beast hung, hitting it as hard as he could with his shoulder as a distraction. He thumped into its solid flesh. It was four times the size of the one from this morning—likely because it'd already eaten—and it whirled to face him as he landed, just as Andi let out a shriek of surprise, jerking the door closed behind her.

Relief swept through him. She was inside the room now; he could see her behind the lurker, and the other staff was harvesting the gear from the cart she'd brought, but her hands were on the glass door, and her dark eyes were on him.

The lurker dropped to the ground in front of him, spinning neatly in midair to land on all four feet, sweeping out with its prehensile tail and tongue like some kind of blue demented sea star.

He shrugged out of his coat and tossed it aside, circling the beast, keeping its attention on him. "You know you're going to lose, right?"

The thing howled subsonically and tensed, preparing to attack.

Damian let his dragon surge just beneath the surface and felt it match him, hungry for battle. He shrugged as he cracked his neck. "All right, then. It's your funeral."

The lurker charged, and so did he.

ANDI STOOD STARING out at Damian facing off with the lurker like they were in some weird sci-fi Western mash-up, her fists curled helplessly against the glass.

He just saved my life—again.

Andi had a faint idea that it might not be okay to be in a relationship where you could lose track of how often the other person had saved your life, but none of that mattered right now—not when Damian was out there, and there was nothing she could do to help him.

"Andi! Epi!"

Reality landed like a ten-ton weight, and she took in everything at once. The monitor in the room was blaring all sorts of warnings, while people she knew delivered CPR and had an ambu bag giving whoever was on the bed 100% oxygen.

"On it!" she shouted, not even knowing who she was shouting it to, only that it was her job to fucking find some. She ripped through the drawers of the crash cart, breaking open all the locks until she found a syringe and cued it up. "Access?"

"Right AC!" Of course, Sheila was there. She was the nurse most likely to be assigned charge any night she was on because, in a field of bossy women, she was best at it.

Something heavy crashed outside. The floor trembled. An inhuman sound, almost like laughter, cut through the noise of the monitors.

Focus. She had to focus.

Andi danced around the right side of the bed with the epinephrine and a saline flush and realized that she knew the patient too. *Jessica? Fuck!* She ran the epi through and flushed it, while Matt kept pushing and counting. "What happened?" she asked, racing back to the cart to queue up a second dose.

"Good...fucking...question," Matt said, in between pumps of CPR.

"Giant blue thing. Some kind of demon," Sheila said, surveilling everything while playing with the cross on her necklace. "Rhythm check!" she shouted, and Matt pulled back.

"It says if we don't get her to OR, none of this is going to fucking count," Ishita said from the front of the bed, momentarily holding the bag off of Jessica's face so that the EKG machine would track Jessica's heart—and only Jessica's heart. The woman on the bed was broken; anyone could see that—one femur was snapped, her shoulder was dislocated, and part of her skull was dented in. It was like something had picked her up and thrown her around like a rag doll—and Andi was guessing something had.

"Matt, tap out," Sheila commanded. The rhythm on the monitor was still ominous, and while everyone here knew they were fighting a losing battle, no one wanted to give up.

"No!" He fought her.

Andi grabbed his shoulders and bodily pulled him back. "I'm fresh," she said, jumping on the bedframe to start CPR.

That monster did this, Andi had time to think while she pulsed. *The monster that is still outside. With Damian.* She tried to focus on what she was doing, keep her speed up, keep counting, keep making sure the strokes were deep enough to matter.

"Oh fuck, that thing is back!" Ishita yelped from the head of the bed.

Andi fought not to look. If she did, she'd get distracted, and then she wouldn't be doing Jessica any good.

"More epi!" Sheila commanded, and Matt rushed in to give it.

"Who the fuck is that out there with him?" he said from his vantage point on Andi's left.

Andi bit her lips. *Don't look, don't look, just pump.*

"There's no one," Ishita said, then paused. "Holy shit."

"Right?" Matt agreed, then full body winced as he saw a blow outside land. "Fuck," he said in a guttural voice, and it took all of Andi's strength not to look. She segued into a *Please be okay, please be okay*, instead.

"Rhythm check!" Sheila shouted. Andi paused, hands hovering just off of Jessica's chest. "Shit, it's shockable. Everyone back!"

Andi jumped off the bed and stared outside, listening to the ascending scale of the defibrillator's charge. The blue monster was pacing back down the hall and away from their room as though he were being lured, but where was Damian? Why couldn't she see him? She held her breath. Jessica was dying no matter what the monitor said. Her stomach was starting to swell—either her injuries had caused a bleed or CPR had. It happened. You couldn't just punch organs with enough strength to move blood and not cause collateral damage. And who the hell knew what her intracranial pressure was with that skull fracture—had anyone checked her eyes? Andi could already taste the acid at the back of her throat, the familiar sensation of knowing she was going to fail, no matter how hard she tried.

"I'm clear, you're clear, we're all clear! Shocking!" Sheila said, waving a hand over Jessica's body like an assistant in a magic act, then hit the button to deliver the charge. The rhythm on the monitor jumped and Matt lunged in, feeling for a pulse because just because your heart was beating didn't mean that it was working right.

A heart could beat, but not have enough blood to pump.

"Nothing," Matt announced. They'd exhausted all the resources in the room and crash cart. They'd poured liters of fluid into her, but saline couldn't replace the red stuff.

"I could," Andi offered, gesturing to the door.

"Don't you dare," Sheila said. "No one's committing suicide on my watch."

"I can take the stairs; I know the back way," Andi said, edging around her. Matt had already jumped back on the bed to restart CPR. Then Sheila's eyes widened, looking at something behind her, and Andi whirled around. The blue thing was back, missing one of its legs, yet still managing to skitter on its remaining three, racing right for them.

"No, no, no, no, no," Ishita intoned, as though her words could ward the monster off—when Andi saw the only thing that possibly could.

"Damian." She breathed his name and stepped up closer to the glass. The second he was done, she could run for the blood bank. He hadn't saved her life this many times already to let anything happen to her now.

The monster leapt onto the glass right in front of her, and she gasped as the force of it shook the window in its hinges. And then *he* was there, wrapping his arms around its torso like in a wrestling show, prying it off—leaving the glass to rattle as he twisted it to the ground—and put a knee in its back to pin it as he changed his grip to encompass its neck and squeeze. It thrashed beneath him, boneless as far as she could tell, especially by the way all its limbs rehinged to claw back at him, ripping through his shirt and against his skin, making him bleed more of his strange green blood. Andi gasped and tears sprang to her eyes.

She wanted to beat her hands against the glass, to tell him that she was there, that she was witnessing him do this, to let him know that he wasn't going through the pain that she could clearly see written across his face alone. But she didn't want to distract him, and he didn't look up or over at her—not until the thing was dead, its blue corpse sagging to the ground as he dropped it—just as she heard the monitor on the crash cart behind her sing the monotonous note that meant Jessica was gone too.

Andi twisted back for a moment, looking at her fallen coworker —definitely wanting to cry—and then looked back outside where Damian stood, panting, the bottom half of his T-shirt ripped away, with gouges leaking green across his chest.

"Who...the...fuck...is...that?" Matt demanded, still doing CPR.

"I'm calling it," Sheila said. "Stand down."

Andi swallowed and put a hand to the glass, waiting for Damian to look up—worried that he wouldn't, that he'd just turn and walk down the hall and leave all of this in her memories. And then with a deep inhale, he did, looking up as though seeing her for the first time, and he smirked, leaning over to match her hand with his much bigger one, smeared with blue and green.

She shoved the door open. This time no one was going to be able to stop her.

CHAPTER NINETEEN

"Are you all right?" she breathed, taking him and the monster he'd killed in, then looking back into the room she'd just been in.

He ignored her question and asked his own. "Are you?"

Andi didn't think she knew the answer to that right now. "Yes... no...maybe?"

"Come with me," he said, gesturing her forward with both hands. She took a step and then he picked her up and over the monster's corpse, setting her down on the far side.

"Damian...you..." she tried again, reaching for his stomach where his beautiful abs had been slashed repeatedly.

"Don't worry about me." He caught one of her hands before she could touch him. "This is just my usual Saturday night," he said, and pulled her down the hall, sweeping his coat up on the way.

They ran into the last ICU room and found Austin there—and Zach—covered in even more blood, but this time it was red.

"What happened?" Damian demanded the second they were inside.

"I'm sorry, I couldn't stop it, and I couldn't leave him. There are

Hunters here," Austin was saying, as she ran up to Zach's bedside. He was torn up again, having given birth to the latest monstrosity. It looked like a war zone.

"How the fuck is he even alive?" she whispered, looking between the men. "Like, is he part zombie?" She dodged around Austin and dialed the blood pressure medications up. Jessica...was dead. She wasn't her favorite coworker by any stretch, but that didn't mean she deserved to die.

Maybe Damian could do something to save her? He knew magic or something, right?

"What are you doing?" Austin asked from his position beside Zach, where he was holding pressure on him again.

"Postponing the inevitable, I hope," she said, folding up her panic and putting it into a mental box. She'd just cranked up all the medication that might help. "The blood bank's on the third floor, I can go—"

"No, you can't," Damian said, grabbing her arm to stop her before looking at Austin. "How much longer?"

Austin glanced at his wrist. "Five minutes. Does he have that, with all those?" he asked, eyeing the pumps.

Andi looked up at the monitor and felt her nursely exterior sliding back into place. Somehow Zach's numbers weren't plummeting downward, not like they ought to be—if she'd lost as much blood as was on this floor now, she'd be dead for sure. So there was some other element she didn't know at play here. "I don't know, I'm not God, but maybe?"

"All right, good," Austin said, then he stared at Damian. "She shouldn't be here."

"Fuck. You," Andi told him and reached to take Zach's pulse. She could see it on the monitor, but she needed to feel it—skin to skin— to actually believe he had one.

Damian grabbed her hand before she touched him. "Don't. If that's real silver, you'll hurt him." He held her hand up so that she could see her bracelet and rings. "Tell me everything," he asked

Austin, releasing her.

"He was fine until an orderly came in and started poking at him," Austin said. "Waving something over him? Short guy? Bald? Had full sleeve tattoos."

Andi cut him off. "But we don't have orderlies on our floor." One of the hazards of being an ICU nurse—better patient ratios, but less ancillary staff to help.

Austin's jaw clenched, and he looked to Damian again. "Then it was Hunters for sure. I knew it. That guy set all this off. Goddammit, D, this is why I told you the hospital was a bad idea—"

"Fine, we'll install some sort of blood bank at the castle for the next time someone has a portal open in them. Oh, wait, that's never fucking happened before." Damian's voice was low and pissed off as Andi's mind started to churn.

"I know, I know," Austin said, his tone an apology. "But how the fuck, D—"

"What do portals look like?" Andi blurted out. Both of the men turned to look at her. "I think I saw it. This morning." The thing that had glinted in Zach's belly before being submerged in blood. Maybe she hadn't imagined it—maybe it was real.

Damian grabbed her shoulders. "What did you see?"

She thought back quickly. "It was shiny like mirror glass—like a little piece of mylar."

"An implanted portal mirror? Impossible," Austin said.

"And yet, here we are," Damian said to himself. Underneath the tatters of his T-shirt, his skin was healing—nearly whole—but she still wanted to touch it to make sure. He frowned in thought, then reached a hand out to her as if he'd read her mind, and she bit her lips. "Give me your bracelet, Andi."

She inhaled to ask why but didn't for once, as she took it off and handed it over. Its silver didn't seem to hurt him as he bent it straight like a blade.

"Austin, get back," Damian warned.

The other man stood his ground. "No. We're just two minutes away now—"

"From that thing being stuck inside him again, and who knows when this all repeats itself," Damian said, advancing on the bed.

"Maybe he'll heal it out!"

"Who knows how long it's been there? It's coming out tonight. This is too much chaos to clean up a third time." Damian pushed Austin aside, and Zach started freely bleeding again. Andi gasped and ran to the IV pumps to dial all of the medications higher, ignoring all the warning alarms. "If he dies, it's better his death is on me than you," Damian said, deciding.

"I can touch it if I put on gloves!" Austin said, running for the boxes on the walls. "I can do it!"

"Do...do what?" Andi twisted back, clearly missing some vital piece. But then, in a moment of horrible clarity, she understood, because Damian was holding her bracelet up like a scalpel and bringing it inexorably down to Zach's abdomen. "Oh my God, you're going to hurt him, aren't you?" Andi whirled back to the remaining IV pumps—one of them was fentanyl—and she cranked it up. "Do you even know what you're doing?"

"Yes. Do you?" Austin challenged her—no, he was challenging Damian—and his voice was low and full of menace that hadn't been there just before. Something about the man had changed. He was bigger—how?—and his clothes were tighter, and his wristwatch's band snapped. It didn't make sense to her, but then nothing for the last three hours really had, had it? She bit her lips to keep her panic to herself, and focused on Damian instead.

"Let me do it," she demanded, stopping his hand with her own.

Damian looked at her darkly. "It's not safe."

"None of tonight has been safe!" Her hand clenched around his. He would have to pry her off to continue. "And medical procedures aren't safe. That's why generally you get people's permission before doing them!"

"We don't have time," Damian growled.

"He was my patient last night, and he's still my patient now. You will have to hurt me before I let you hurt him," she hissed.

"You don't know what you're getting into," Damian protested.

She was using all of her strength against him and she hadn't even made him budge. It wasn't fair—it would have to be words or nothing. "But I do. This is my job, remember? I've had way more experience at this kind of thing than you. So let me help."

He was an immovable mountain determined to not let her pass, and his eyes were glazed over. Even though he was looking right at her, she knew he couldn't see her—he was looking too hard into his past.

"Just trust me, Damian," she whispered.

His attention snapped to the here and now. She thought she saw a stricken look on his face, but then it was gone as if it had never been there.

"Just this once," she promised.

His golden gaze poured over her, and then it was like he was seeing her again—here, in the flesh, beside him—and he swallowed. "Okay," he said, relenting. He passed the bracelet over. "Do you remember where it was?"

"I really fucking hope so," Andi muttered, pulling all of her silver rings off to throw them to the ground.

TOGETHER THEY WORKED ON ZACH. She cut the delicate tissues keeping loops of bowel in place with her bracelet's edge, attempting to avoid arteries and organ damage. Damian gently pulled the looping organ out of him, putting it in a messy pile beside Zach's hips as they gutted him like a Halloween pumpkin. Austin breathed down their necks the entire time.

Where had she seen that glimmer earlier? Was it even there? What if it'd been some sleepless trick of her imagination? What if Zach died right now—because of her? After seeing Jessica die, she couldn't fucking take that. And how the shit-fuck-hell were they going to get all of these pieces back inside the man? Just because she wasn't a butcher didn't mean she was a surgeon. And none of this shit was sterile and…and…and…

"You've got this. It's okay," Damian told her.

She didn't dare look over at him.

"Keep going." He put his hand on hers, and she found the strength to go on.

"Moon's nigh," Austin growled. "Step away before—"

"I'm not losing him," Damian said. Oh God, how many times had she heard doctors say that right before they did lose someone?

"But you lost Michael," Austin went on, and it was like he was speaking around too many teeth.

Andi tugged up one more layer. She'd torn a small artery, so the basin of Zach's abdomen was filling up with a slow bleed, but… "Oh my God," she whispered, as something small and silver glimmered inside of him like a fish.

"Found it." Damian's hand darted into Zach and lifted a small-shining-something the size of a half-dollar before ripping it into shreds—right before Austin's fallen wristwatch began alarming. Damian's expression stayed intense as he took two quick steps away from the bed—even though Zach looked like half of an all-you-can-eat cannibal buffet. *What the fuck?*

"Moon's full," he told her before she could ask like that was an explanation. "Either it works or it doesn't."

That made absolutely no sense to her. "We can't just leave him like that!" She ran for the bed, and Damian caught her, picking her up and turning her around so that her back was to the bed.

"Don't look!" he commanded sharply as she tried to turn her head.

Andi obeyed him but only barely, especially when worrisomely disgusting sounds began behind her. "Why?" she asked in a hiss.

Damian brought his forehead to hers to trap it, his golden eyes shining bright. "Do you ever stop with the questions, princess?"

She shook her head, rocking it against his. "No. Never." And then she winced as it sounded like bones began to break, accompanied by a wet slurping that had no place in a hospital. He closed his eyes as if in prayer, and then when the sounds stopped he rose up to look, and it was like she saw a mighty weight lifted from his shoulders in real time, as he happily sighed.

"Okay," Damian breathed, before giving her a triumphant grin. "It's over. Don't scream."

Andi slowly turned around, like a contestant on a game show nervous to see what she'd won. Both men were gone, and in their place were two motherfuckingly huge wolves now panting behind her. Each of them was the size of a couch, wide shouldered but lean and long from nose to tail-tip. One of them had the same rust colored fur as Austin's hair in mottled splotches across its body as it shook its shaggy head, and the other was an almost scatter-camouflage combination of white, black, and gray.

Damian walked over to them like he knew them because—she realized—he did. "I'm glad to see you back in one piece," he addressed the one that had to be Zach. "I don't know what the fuck you did to yourself, though. We'll figure it out later—when you can talk." He then went over to the sink and started washing his hands.

They were werewolves.

Her hands. Were covered. In werewolf blood.

Andi pressed them away from her, holding them out at arm's length. Zach's wolf whined while Austin's gnashed its teeth at Damian, before giving her a baleful look.

"Yeah, I know," Damian answered in response, like he understood them, drying his hands off before pulling out his phone. "Max is already on his way."

Andi didn't care who the fuck Max was right now; she couldn't take much more strange tonight. "So...Austin...and Zach are werewolves?" Her voice went high as she said it aloud because it was so dang crazy, and yet here they were, carnivores the size of pro-linebackers, and she was close enough to see their claws and fangs. She skittered around the edge of the room to where the sink was, and then Austin growled. She quickly stepped to hide behind Damian.

"Well, I can hardly deny it when she's standing right here, gentlemen," Damian said. "Plus, she's saved your life twice now, Zach. That's a blood debt. If you ask me, you both owe her."

Andi tried to wash her hands super thoroughly without turning her back on the two massive killing machines, and it was hard—especially when the gray one shuffled around Damian to look at her more clearly. Its eyes were blue and piercing under an intelligent brow.

"Zach, Andi. Andi, Zach," Damian said.

What were you supposed to do when you were introduced to a werewolf? Andi thought of curtsying and then stopped from manically laughing at herself but only barely.

"Hi puppy," she squeaked instead.

Damian laughed. "Wait until I tell Grim that."

Andi tentatively reached her hand out, and Damian's mood changed. "What do you think you're doing?" he snapped. She yanked her hand back and held it to her chest like it was wounded.

"Petting a werewolf? Maybe? Should I have asked for permission first? I don't know."

"You don't pet werewolves," Damian said, every word punctuated with disbelief.

"Why not?"

He blinked at her. "Because...they're...they're monsters."

Zach went down on all fours like the world's largest stuffed wolf and let his tongue loll out as if to debate that fact.

"So?" she asked, biting her lips and creeping up on Zach slowly. His ears were as big as her hands, and they looked so soft.

"They're also men, the vast majority of the time. Just because they're fuzzy now, don't let it fool you."

Andi crossed her arms. "So, it was entirely okay for me to have my hands in Zach's guts when he was a man a few minutes ago, but right now, I can't pet him?"

Austin gnashed his teeth at her as if to emphasize this point, whereas Zach sat back, and...beat his tail. Which was intentionally doglike, if you asked her. His brother looked utterly disgusted with him. Damian yanked the room's curtains shut and sat on the visitor couch, closing his eyes. Which meant he wouldn't see if she pet Zach. She leaned out and Damian spoke up again, without looking. "Don't."

"Don't what?" she asked, not moving.

"Don't think that I don't know what you're doing," he answered her.

"But..." she protested.

Damian's golden eyes opened and took all of her in. "I need to think, and I'm tired of words."

ALL HE WANTED WAS *a moment to himself.* Just one moment, to clear his head and think things through—and somehow stay angry. At her. Because everything about her made him weak. He was angry that she'd seen him for what he was and hadn't run, angry that he wanted to let her in, angry that all of his attempts to frighten her away tonight hadn't done a fucking thing—not even when she'd almost died from a lurker. She should be cowering somewhere, mind broken, utterly panicked, begging him to take her home—not trying to pet his werewolf best friend like he was some goddamned Fido.

But she couldn't even give him that—*because of course she couldn't, when had she ever done anything easily?*—and he opened his eyes up and saw her standing there looking bereft.

There, he had what he wanted. Right?

Zach cocked an eyebrow at him meaningfully.

Goddammit.

Damian moved over on the couch. "Come here, Andi."

Her eyes narrowed. "Do you think you can just order me around all the time?"

"NOW," he barked.

She didn't move a muscle. She really wasn't going to listen to him. He was tempted to lunge over the wolves and pick her up to get her away from them and then do whatever the fuck he wanted to her, but instead, he collapsed dramatically backward and clutched at his rib cage.

"Damian?" Her voice rose in an arc of worry as she rushed to his side.

"It's just...I...," he said, mock-groaning as her hands fluttered, chasing his. Up close, she smelled amazing, and then her hands were on his chest and he wanted them elsewhere—wanted more of everything with her—and he forgot to keep up the act.

"You!" she shouted, shoving at him the second she realized.

"I did hurt there. For a second," he lied, smirking.

God, she smelled so *right*. And an unwise part of him wanted to wrap her in his arms, to just breathe her in, and know that she was whole and okay. He snuck his arm around her waist, ready to hold onto her if she tried to move away.

"Just...stay away from the wolves, okay? They have more teeth than sense."

She rocked away and stopped touching him, but she didn't stand up. "I'm getting a strong current of pot-kettle-black here."

He snorted. "Good, because I'd tell you the same thing about my dragon. We share the same body, but he isn't me. And he's not pettable, either."

Why not? his dragon asked him.

Not-the-fuck-now, Damian replied, making sure that none of his internal exchange showed upon his face.

"If he's not you, then who is he?" Andi asked, her brow furrowing.

Damian closed his eyes and groaned in pain for real this time. "It's too complicated..."

And when he opened his eyes, she was frowning at him again. "Why won't you ever answer anything?"

"Because, princess, just because," he answered like that was enough, although from her expression it clearly wasn't. She was so close beside him now and his body roared to move against hers. His arm was already looped behind her; it would be nothing to scoop her into his lap and hold her there—pressed against him. How come her presence—*the very smell of her, even!*—kept clouding his mind like some kind of drug, making him hyperaware of her proximity at all times, and aching for his next hit? No one had ever made him feel like that before—which was yet another reason to be angry.

Because this was not who he was. He was Damian Blackwood, in control of himself and his dragon—always, completely—at all times. If he lost control, people died.

But he reached out against all of his better judgment and stroked the blue streak in her hair off her cheek and back behind her ear. Her eyes were wide, and her lips were parted, and all of this was her fault somehow. Even if she wasn't doing it on purpose, it was still happening. He had to get away from her—or closer, now, dear God, *yes*—there was no in-between.

Then he heard a sound coming to save him. Maximillian and his Forgetting Fire. Damian dropped his hand, back to business, and ignored the noises coming from the wolves that sounded suspiciously like laughter.

"About damn time," Damian said, standing suddenly, leaving her hanging again. Andi fought not to sway. He'd wanted to kiss her, and she didn't know what she wanted, but she hadn't really wanted to stop him, and then a switch inside him flipped. How could he turn himself on and off like that? He was glowering now and Andi wondered if he even realized when he did it, or if being the definition of mercurial was just his natural state.

There was a crackling sound outside—increasing in volume—like either a giant was tramping through a forest, or the whole building was on fire. She kept expecting to hear a Code Red announced as the crackling sound got louder, passed them, presumably reached the end of the hall, then turned back before silencing right outside their door.

There was a rap on the glass. "Damian?"

"We need at least two spheres in here, but I'll take four if you've got them," Damian said, loud enough to be heard. The glass door slid open, and four marble sized things rolled in.

Damian picked up all of them and held out two in one palm toward the wolves. They each daintily took one into their mouths, and as they did so, Andi watched them completely disappear and she yelped in surprise. Damian ignored her. "You can come in now, Max."

The door opened all the way, but there was no one there. Just the hallway.

"A...ghost?" she guessed aloud. She knew there was such a thing as werewolves now, so why the fuck not?

"No, spheres. A magical object that protects the outside world from seeing us." Damian handed one over to her and she took it. She didn't feel any different, but now she could see the wolves again, and the ghost turned out to be a very-pale skinned man, clad mostly in black leather, who had what looked like welders goggles on over a mohawk of ice blond hair that wasn't spiked but rested to one side like Death's horse's mane. He held out a lantern that had all its windows covered—for now.

A second later, Damian joined them there, in their hidden world just under other people's noses. Maximillian coughed and not-so-subtly swung his lantern in Andi's direction. Damian shook his head. "Get the boys home and stay out of trouble. Hunters might be present."

"Understood," Maximillian said with a nod, then opened the door again. The wolves ran out under fluorescent lights, their claws clicking on the linoleum tile, even more improbable outside the room than they'd been inside it. Zach looked back at her and gave her a short *ayoo* as she waved helplessly at him. Without him here to distract her, everything was real again. And it was all going to really hit her—soon.

Damian turned. "This is your floor, right?"

After everything she'd seen tonight, she wasn't sure anymore. "It was," she answered.

He gave her a suggestive look. "Can I borrow some bath wipes?"

Andi blinked. Was he being serious? After all that?

"I mean, if you didn't use them all up on your doctor friends," he went on.

She inhaled, thought about hitting his arm hard, and then settled on saying, "You know there's something wrong with you, right?"

"It's called being incorrigible," he said. "Come on, where's your locker?"

CHAPTER
TWENTY

They stepped out into the ICU together, and everything was normal. Doors were open, beds were where they belonged, and staff and patients were carrying on like nothing had happened.

"Can they hear us?" she whispered while directing him to the locker room.

"No."

"Will they see if I open the door?" It was nightshift. If things were back to normal, she could guarantee that someone was sleeping in the dark on break.

"Not if they want to see darkness."

"Okay, that's so confusing, but anyway." She gave up and went inside. He followed her and sure enough, three of her coworkers were stretched out on couches or chains of chairs, snoozing. She opened her locker to rummage through her bag and gave him the first handful.

"Thanks," he said, wiping himself down, starting with his hair. She looked him up and down, telling herself she was being professional, merely trying to assess if he had suffered any injuries that hadn't healed and needed to be cared for. But the bottom of his shirt had been torn off, revealing those insane rippling abs. "Are you going to?" he asked her, gesturing with his hand at her. "I mean, I can help if you want," he said with a leer.

Andi swallowed and hopped back. "I'm good. It's just...silk and bath wipes...don't mix, I think."

"Of course," he said sarcastically.

She wasn't the one covered in monster blood—just her coat was. If only she'd known that this was going to happen before she'd dropped that hundred-dollar bill for dry cleaning on the ground at Belissima's. She snorted and turned to look at her coworkers in an effort not to look at him. How had they missed all the excitement outside? Nightshift's abilities to sleep on breaks were legendary, but come the fuck on. Then realization hit her. "Wait, was that Forgetting Fire in the lantern? Like you wanted to show me?"

He slowly nodded. "Yes."

"And it did...all this?" She gestured at her coworkers, who were all sleeping like serfs at Sleeping Beauty's castle.

"Yes," he agreed.

It was like it had undone time! "Oh, thank God!" Andi leaned against her locker and heard it click. "Jessica's back, right?"

Damian frowned, shaking his head as he finished rubbing a hand across his stomach. "No."

"What do you mean, no? Can't you...bring her back?"

His countenance changed when his eyes met hers, and it was like he was made out of steel again. "I can't. That's not how it works."

"But...she was here. People will remember—"

"Yes. And they'll find her car in the parking lot. I assume they track your badges, so they'll know that she got in, but they won't have a record of her dying, nor will anyone have much of a memory of her working here tonight. That's what happens when you die for Unearthly reasons. Most human minds can't handle it." He finished wiping off his forearms and shoved the stained wipes in his pocket.

"But...there are cameras!" Andi protested. The woman had kids, for Christ's sake!

"The fire will have gotten to them, too. And in a week, it'll be another unsolved mystery." He raked his eyes over her, taking in her surprise and pain with a sympathetic frown. "Death is death, Andi. Not even I can change it."

"But—" she whispered, and he cut her off.

"For what it's worth, I'm sorry," he said, then pressed on. "Are you all right?"

"No." She was not all right. Not in a global sense, knowing all the shit she now knew about his world, and definitely not in the here and now. Andi stared past him for a moment. "But I'm really good at compartmentalizing, so I figure I've got three or so hours before everything sinks in and I lose it."

Damian appraised her and seemed to take her statement at face value. "Fair enough. Let me get you home."

They rode the elevator down in silence, but Damian held the 'closed' button down before it landed. "Pocket your sphere."

"Why?" she asked, as she did as she was told.

"Because I want to make sure the cameras down here see us leaving," Damian said, letting the button go and zipping up his coat to hide everything that'd happened to his T-shirt.

She dropped the metal ball into her coat pocket and put on a brave smile as they approached the security kiosk.

"Leaving so soon, Miss Ngo?" Omar asked.

"Turns out my friend's not feeling well, and the ICU has more staff than they can handle. That's what happens when you offer double time!" She forced herself to laugh and shrug playfully as Omar let them out the door.

· · ·

Andi followed Damian back to his car and got in without talking. It was her turn to be tired of words and think.

She had just seen the literal definition of too much. Up until now, she'd have thought it was that time she'd had a Steven Johnson's patient's colon slide right out of their body, semi-intact, before popping open and spilling shit everywhere. She'd called in sick for three nights after that, but tonight had that night beat—hands down.

And Damian had understood that. It was why he'd been cruel to her at the restaurant and why he was driving her back home in silence now.

"I get why you push people away," she said aloud. This...was his life. What had happened today was his actual, normal Saturday.

He kept driving like he didn't hear her until he downshifted like mad, surprising her by pulling over underneath an overpass in the dark, with only the dim light of the dashboard for illumination. Andi could hear each of the cars passing overhead and feel the vibration of the bridge as it shook from them.

Damian looked over at her, his face framed in the dark. "Do you?"

He did what he did, although clearly it tormented him, and stopped him from ever letting himself relax. The only doctor she'd ever trusted had told her a wise thing once—that every person who practices war or medicine has a little graveyard somewhere inside of them they visit, full of all the ghosts of their what-ifs. She knew she visited one inside of her from time to time, when she was feeling broken, like nothing she did at work mattered.

But she had a feeling that Damian was trapped in his, with gates he'd locked himself—for the world's protection.

"People around me don't tend to live long lives," he told her. He was in three-quarters light, and it was like she could see his own pain casting him in shadow. "I should've never picked you up. Even at the bus stop, I knew you'd be trouble. But I have a habit of playing with fire."

And she could almost feel it in the air around him now. *Caution, girl.* "Comes with the territory, I assume?" she said, purposefully keeping her tone light.

He groaned. "I walked into that one, didn't I?"

"Pretty much," she said, thinking about him as he tried not to look at her. How could he do what he did and continue? No wonder he was haunted by a pervasive sense of loss. A thing that both of them had in common—at least tonight.

Andi put her hand on his wrist. "You did save me," she told him.

"Of course. What am I, some kind of monster?" Damian gave her a feral smile in the dark. And then he looked at her and then to where they were touching, where she could feel his skin against hers, burning hot, and she remembered reaching up to touch his dragon. He slowly turned toward her, reaching for her, giving her ample opportunity to push him away.

"I should let you go," he said, his voice low.

"Then do it," she whispered back, even as she felt her own heat rising.

His hand clenched her wrist tighter, and then without thinking, she was kicking her shoes off and flowing over her seat toward him, silk whispering against the leather. He pulled back to pull her in on top of him, taking her onto his lap, his hands around her waist, his lips against her hair, until she looked up and saw him waiting, watching, taking all of her in.

"You know you're an arrogant asshole, right?"

"You ask too many questions, princess," he whispered with a grin, half a second before his lips met hers.

His hands swam up the outside of her dress as his tongue pressed in, unbuckling her coat, and the only reason any of this even vaguely worked inside the sports car was because she was so small. Her coat fell against the steering wheel, then down, and he reached around her to pull the lever to push his seat all the way back, stretching him out and laying them both down. She went with him, her mouth still searching his like she was trying to drink him up, and as one of his hands brushed over her silk-covered breast, she paused to moan.

His other hand wound into her hair and pulled her up from him as he kissed down her throat and she froze on top of him. There was something dangerous in that—how close his mouth was to her pulse, and how fragile she knew she was compared to him. She'd been with other men before, of course, and many of them had been stronger than she was, but none of them had ever been predators. Not like he was.

Then Damian's mouth found the spot behind her ear and kissed her there, and she shuddered—came to life again—her hands caressing his abs so artfully exposed by his torn shirt.

He growled comfortably against her and bit her nearest dress strap in two. The other one he just broke with his hand, and he pushed the silk off of her, to pool about her waist. His hands moved over her ribs and breasts, taking the measure of her body. She breathed with each stroke, as she became electrified.

"That's not fair," she said softly, looking down at him—part of his shirt was still on. She hadn't gotten skin earlier in the restaurant, and she wanted it desperately. She needed to feel his hot body—in all senses of the term—pressed against her. She wanted him to warm her from the night, and erase everything she'd been afraid of earlier.

"Life isn't fair," he said, but reached up for his own shirt collar, ripping the cotton off easily and arching up to pull it away. Andi put both her hands on his chest then and felt the swell of muscles there—skin just as hot as she'd imagined. She tilted her head lower to listen, but he knew what she was doing and caught her first. "Don't. I can't afford to have a heart."

She tilted her head back and looked up his chest at him. He was breathing heavily enough to rock her—like waves on the ocean.

"Okay," Andi whispered and lowered her mouth to kiss his chest.

Damian's hands moved against her then—one low and one high.

The low one sinking under the last of her dress to cup at her ass, the high one pulling up between them to cup her breast in its palm—stroking it, gently pulling at her nipple—as her mouth wound up his chest, her sliding herself against him. He groaned as her tongue licked up his clavicle, and he leaned down to catch her mouth again. His hands abandoned her body and tangled themselves in her hair, pulling her into his mouth, showing her what he wanted to do to her there, probing her deeply with his tongue, taking control just as fast as she relinquished it. She moaned into his mouth, and his hands flowed down her, pulling her against him even though her legs were still sidesaddle and closed, asking her, begging her, to open up. One of his hands slid between her legs, catching what little remained of her dress, to start rubbing her with its silk.

She could've easily remained there—his hand was so skilled—she caught his wrist and ground it into her, but she knew she wouldn't be satisfied. Not when so much more was so close. Andi turned toward him, grabbing his shoulders with both hands, using his body to pull herself up, the remaining silk of her skirt rising to let her legs slide astride him, feeling him rock beneath her in anticipation, no matter the fact that his jeans were still on.

"Yes," he whispered, catching her up with one arm and easily holding her there, kissing her breasts as they presented to him, sucking at each of her hard nipples, as his free hand navigated his belt and jeans below. He rippled beneath her rather like a snake, and she knew that he was free and that all she had to do was to carefully slide back down, where she would find him—hard and ready—below. She knew she didn't need to look, that her body would perfectly fit him—this evening's time at the restaurant had proven that—but she paused, waiting, and she didn't know why.

"I shouldn't want you," she whispered, even as the heat in her kept growing, knowing that he was so hard, so close.

Damian brought his hand up to hold her cheek. "No, princess, you shouldn't."

There were some words when you hear them, you instantly know that they are true—even if you want to pretend that they are not. Andi saw it at the hospital all the time—patients fighting against dire diagnoses—in part because on some level they knew that they were truthful and that doctors wouldn't lie.

You didn't fight against what you didn't believe in.

And so, she knew the truth when she heard it coming from Damian's mouth. He was a dangerous man—and also a massive and horrific beast—and there was no way any part of this was right or safe, and they both knew that.

But nothing on this world—or any of the others—could stop her from sliding down.

Everything stilled waiting on her, and for the first time since they'd started making out, Andi could hear the cars flying by above again—making the bridge echo with their passage one by one—and somewhere under the remnants of her skirt her thighs were parted, and she was ready to take him in, sight unseen. She found him—or he found her—and she pressed against him and she heard him moan, just as she did, both of them feeling her begin to part around him.

"Oh, Andi," he whispered, his hands tightening around her waist, barely stopping himself from dragging her onto him.

And slowly, in time with the beating of the cars driving above, she began to find a rhythm, rising and lowering, entirely in control of her own ride. He hissed with anticipation each time she lowered to take more of him in, and he groaned when she rose up too high, leaving him bereft—and then slowly, almost so slowly she didn't notice it was happening, he began to move with her too, stroking into her in her own time, until she was as low as she could be, stretched totally around him, and he was hilt deep inside.

It was the final line of her invitation to him. He grabbed her ass, pulled her close, and started to thrust in earnest and then she couldn't hear the cars anymore over their own sounds—the way she moaned when he filled her, the way he was breathing rough, the slick-perfect-wetness of the place where they met—again and again. He used an arm to push himself up, crushing her to him with his other one, kissing anything he could reach—hard—pinning her on him again and again, her thighs wide, her clit grinding against his perfect abs—and then he paused, falling back on the seat behind him, breathing hard, staring up at her like she was a goddess.

"Show me how to make you come," he said, his voice low and serious.

"What?" Andi laughed nervously, her voice rising.

His hands caught her hips again and rocked her back and forth. "There's no room in here for me to eat you out again." He held her still and slowly thrust up into her, reminding her of how far they'd already come. "And I have to see you—feel you—come again. I have to."

She looked down at him, panting, wiping her sweaty hair away from her face and breasts with one hand.

There are dragons in this world, my dear. Real dragons.

"Anything that you desire," he said, arching his hips into a slow stroke.

To know a dragon is to be cursed.

"Name it, princess," he growled, rocking deep in her once more.

Beware.

"No," she said aloud, throwing her head back, chasing Auntie Kim's warning from her mind. Andi looked down and saw the determination in his eyes, felt the heat of his hands on her ass, and the way that his cock throbbed inside her as she slid herself up and down it. She was in control right now—she was riding him. And even if he was a dragon, he was begging to release *her*. She wasn't going to let any amount of superstition stop her from taking this. "I'll show you."

Damian made an acquiescing rumble deep in his chest.

She leaned down and worked her way up his neck to kiss on him the spot she wanted to be kissed on, the spot below her ear that made her go insane, and he chuckled darkly. "Then this," she whispered, taking one of his hands to pull it underneath her breast. He took the hint and kissed at it, looking up.

"And what's next?" he asked, after swiping his tongue across her nipple.

"This, at the end," she said, taking his other hand and bringing his thumb to her mouth, sucking on it to get it wet before pushing it down to where they joined—right beneath her clit—to use it as another point of friction, grinding herself down. He purred at this.

"All right...let me see," Damian said, releasing his hand. He brought her down into his arms and breathed against her ear, licking up its outer shell, before sinking back to kiss the perfect spot, the one that made electricity shudder through her no matter what, so that her thighs clenched and pulsed against him, fluttering in a way she couldn't help.

"Oh, that's delightful," he murmured, doing it again, and then he breathed and licked his way down to pull her nipple into his hot mouth, rolling his tongue across it and sucking hard, while pinching the other, until his mouth and hand were reversed—the heat of his mouth and the heat of his hand were interchangeable, and both of them were stoking a fire she kept secret within her—and he started to thrust into her again with intent. Then he reached up a hand and pressed his thumb into her mouth, to trail it wetly down between her breasts and stomach until she couldn't wait for what was next, settling it between them, rubbing at her as his hips arched up.

She put her hands against his chest and ground on top of him. He curled forward to catch her waist with his free hand, pulling her into him, pushing her hair out of her face to kiss her fiercely, then twining her hair around his hand like a rope, using it to keep her over him—his mouth never stopping, his cock never stopping. Any time she came up for air, she found him almost burning her with his intense golden gaze. Andi started to moan as the fire in her expanded, giving herself over to his relentless onslaught, as he did everything she asked of him, again and again.

Oh God, she was so close. She put a hand out against the low ceiling, pressing herself down even harder so that the movements between them were so subtle—yet sharp—and the friction so hot—his hand, his mouth, her breast, her clit. "Fuck me, oh...Damian... don't stop... just fuck me," she whispered.

"Take what's yours," he commanded in a groan.

Everything inside her tightened up into one impossibly tight clench, and then everything let go. She screamed as she roiled above him, as he didn't stop. He rode her through, into each wave and then out of it again—her entire body alight, bursting with one flame after another—until finally they were quenched and she collapsed above him like a burnt-out star, panting into the vicinity of his neck. "Oh my God," she whispered.

"God has nothing to do with it," Damian said, twisting his head to kiss her forehead.

Damian moved his hands to hold her to him and to stroke her back. He'd been with so many women in his lifetime, but none of them had come for him like that—so completely letting themselves go, holding nothing in reserve. She was gasping on top of him, with him still hard inside her, and even the smallest movements she made were deliciously tortuous. "Shhhhhh," he soothed her and pulled her up so that his cock was free. She moaned at this, unsettled by its absence, and he kissed her cheek.

"You—" she protested.

"Don't worry about me." It was enough to have seen her and felt her explode on him. He would cherish memories of how she looked, how she felt, giving herself over, for decades to come.

She frowned down at him. Any makeup she'd had on earlier had sweated off a long time ago, and yet she was still impossibly beautiful. "I'm a nurse; you can't tell me not to worry. It is literally my job." She reached back with one hand and swirled the remaining silk around her waist up until her hand found his still wet cock and gently took hold.

"Andi," he began, starting her name as a protest, but taking it into a moan. He'd been so close inside her earlier. The only reason he hadn't come was because he'd wanted to fully appreciate her coming—now somehow, as she started stroking, he found himself getting harder still. "I don't want to lose control around you," he admitted quickly as her hand traced its way down his shaft.

"Why not?" she asked, lowering herself down to kiss his chest again.

"You saw the wall at the restaurant. It's not safe."

She paused in kissing, but her hand still stroked. "For me? Or for you?" She leaned over and gently bit his nearest bicep.

He closed his eyes, moaning softly, and then his dragon was there. His dragon had been riding him, close and quiet. In certain ways, these were the only times they overlapped easily, him inside his dragon when it was fighting, and his dragon inside of him when there was sex.

Keep going, his dragon urged him.

And now he would have to talk both of them down, *dammit.* Damian closed his eyes, trying to ignore her touching him.

It's not safe, he explained. And then he showed his dragon a montage of all the times they'd already put Andi in danger tonight.

His dragon was momentarily confused, and as it relented, he somehow found the strength to reach for her wrist to stop her.

"Damian," she whispered, setting her forehead against his. "I need this. Please. Just help me forget everything else a little longer."

She'd come into his life and reached into his chest and had somehow shaken everything up again, bringing things to the surface that he'd forgotten he possessed. How on earth was he supposed to fight her when the thing she wanted most was what he wanted too? She leaned forward against him, enveloping him with her sweet perfume, her hair sliding over them both, her breasts temptingly close to where he could kiss them, her hand still wrapped around his rock-hard cock.

"I know, Andi, but," he began, his voice guttural—and his dragon cut him off.

You would never hurt your mate.

Damian's hand paused in surprise and she took that as permission not to stop.

She's not, he protested.

Can't you feel it? Can't you smell it? his dragon asked.

All he could feel was her hand around him, and how much he yearned to be back inside her. And the entire car smelled like sex, obviously, but something in Andi's scent—the caramel and apples and ocean that he was familiar with—had deepened into a sweet and heady musk—a scent that he would follow anywhere, were it made into perfume.

Don't you know? his dragon pressed, showing him memories from his own mind. The way his chest had tightened when he'd first seen her at the bus stop, how aptly she'd handled Austin and he'd approved, how safe he felt leaving Zach with her—even when she'd operated on him, fucking hell!—and how he hadn't been able to bring himself to steal her memories away when he'd never had any compunction about doing it to others before. And then, at the restaurant, when he'd known he had to have her—everything else be damned. All of it made sense now.

What was happening between them wasn't just lust. It was some strange kind of fate.

Oh...God...yes, he whispered to his dragon in rising horror. *But we can never, ever, tell her,* he told his dragon, as he opened up his eyes and saw Andi smiling softly down. *Promise me.*

His dragon paused again at this, and he felt the confusion

swirling from it before it gave up on trying to understand. *Human words are yours, not mine,* it said. *But we both share this body.*

"I can stop if you want?" she asked, slowing down. She looked as confused as his dragon felt, but he released her arm.

"You make things harder for me," he said hoarsely.

She snorted with a grin. "I don't think you have any problem with that yourself."

No wonder she drove him mad; no wonder being with her felt right. "Hmmmm." He made an accommodating sound and leaned forward until he was almost upright and she was scrambling for purchase. "Here," he said, picking her up and setting her back into her seat gently.

"Damian," she protested, misreading his intent until he reached his hands over to operate the latches on her seat as well, pushing it back and flat just as his seat had been. He finished pushing off his jeans, kicked off his shoes, and then joined her on her side of the car —his hands on either side of her seat, a knee between her legs. She was exposed to him—the perfection of her breasts, the marks he'd left upon them at her urging, the smooth slide of skin down her ribs and across her belly, where the slit in her skirt had rolled over to its most advantageous point and parted to reveal the fine triangle of hair above where they'd so recently been joined.

"You're perfect," he said, trying to memorize her now, to embed an image of her so deep inside that even Forgetting Fire, if it worked on him, wouldn't be able to pull it free.

"Flattery will get you nowhere," she teased, flushing. He could feel the heat of it rising and watched her squirm.

"Is that so?" he asked and moved to kiss her again.

She laced her arms around his neck as he slowly matched himself back to her, chest to chest, hips to hips, his thick cock nudging between her thighs for only a moment before she spread herself as wide as she could for him—given the door nearby—wrapping her legs around him as he slowly sank in. She gasped, and he moaned. How was it possible that being in a woman could feel this good?

Not just any woman, his dragon intoned.

Damian looked down at her, trying to tell if she felt this too, and found her jaw dropped and eyes closed as his cock filled her again. She made a soft sound of satisfaction.

"Okay, I lied – flattery will get you a lot of places, if you keep making me feel like that," she said, reaching up to wind a hand in his hair, opening her eyes to look up at him, bright and wild and ready.

Did she somehow already know too?

He made a triangle of his arms around her, his elbows on the seat above her shoulders, him cradling her head inside his hands as he held her down and kissed her—and then began to thrust.

There was no part of her that did not feel good to him—her mouth, her skin, the way her breasts bobbed against him each time his cock landed—and inside, where her heat enveloped him, so swollen and wet and tight. Every time he pushed in her, he felt like he was breaking new ground, and every time he pulled out the loss of contact with her was too terrible to bear.

Because of this, a primal fear that each stroke might be his last—and because of how goddamned good it felt when she was wrapped around him—he couldn't control himself. His hips started to pick up speed, and she went with him. Each time he landed in her, she made small moans, and each time he pulled out, she gasped until he plunged back inside again. He kissed her mouth fiercely and she met him just the same, her hands curled into his hair to keep his mouth to hers, like she was drinking from him—as his back arched and his hips thrust and her heels drummed against his hips each time he entered her and spread her wide and shoved himself in deep.

And then his vision changed. He wasn't in the dim car anymore, hot over Andi, memorizing her perfection. No, he was flying—with another beast that he couldn't quite see. A glimmer of gold racing off toward the sun. But he knew he longed for it; no, he lusted for it. And he knew it wanted him to chase it back—he wheeled in midair, and then he landed in himself, back with Andi, his body still, him panting wildly.

"Are you okay?" She pushed his hair out of his face, looking up at him with utter concern.

Damian was certain he'd just had a memory of something—only it had never happened to him before.

"Yes," he lied, but it wasn't a lie, really. He was still here, with her—his...mate. She still needed fucking, and he still needed to fuck her. The heat that he'd felt in him as a dragon for that moment still rode him, wracking him with urges meant for monsters instead of men, but his dragon was right. He wouldn't hurt her; he could never hurt her. So, trusting in his dragon, he did as he liked. He moved up to kneeling, grabbed her legs and put one ankle against each shoulder, and then bent back down, plowing harder. He took his thumb and wet it with spit before planting it between her thighs to rub her clit, his other hand holding him up over her so that he didn't crush her entirely, only just the perfect amount, feeling his cock slide into her again and again.

Her hands shot down to hold his wrist on her stomach. "Don't stop...don't stop...don't stop," she breathed.

"Never," he promised, stroking her clit softly, in direct opposition to his rough thrusts.

Her legs tensed against him as if trying to push him back, but he knew it was only her body betraying her, that she was close. Her ankles kicked against him in little flutters, like a cat winding up to pounce. She was breathing hard, biting her lip, and one of her hands was pulling at the opposite breast's nipple and he knew he had her, that he was going to make her fly.

"Oh...please, please." She arced against him—her whole body tense—and then she shouted his name. "Oh my God, Damian! Yes!" as the first wave slammed her, making her shudder and ripple around him.

Yessssssssss, his dragon purred. *NOW*.

His dragon overlapped him, and while he normally would've fought the intrusion, for one singeing-hot moment, it felt right. He thrust in time with the waves of her orgasm, feeling it pull at him like her body needed him to feel whole. He was beyond any point in stopping. Not coming the first time she'd enveloped him with pulses had taken superhuman effort, and neither he nor his dragon had that kind of control anymore.

She writhed again below him, shuddering, one hand curled in his hair against his scalp, whispering, "Please...please..." begging him for his load.

Damian closed his eyes and felt everything in him flood down to where they were joined, where his cock was buried inside her hot throbbing pussy, all of him aching, dying for release.

"Take what's yours," she breathed, just as he had earlier.

And he didn't know if she meant his orgasm or her, but he willed it to be both as he shouted and shot himself inside her.

Damian's hips beat against hers, his body doing what it had to as he came, fucking her hard, grunting, shouting, hissing, as violent pleasures flowed through him, impossibly long, her pussy sucking his hot silver out of him, taking everything he had to give until he was completely dry.

He shifted her legs gently and collapsed on top of her, totally spent, panting into her neck, surrounded by the scent of her skin and hair, his soul still soaring. He felt dizzy, like he was in two places at once—one of him here and the other half of him flying back in the Realms, where his dragon didn't have to worry about being seen—where it could take the purest pleasure in the wind, feeling it thrill against his wings. And then somehow he landed alone back in his Earthly body again, with her wound around him, his softening cock still inside her.

That. That was what it was like to be mated.

What it was always supposed to be like.

Damian swallowed. He knew he needed to recover himself—to somehow go back to being the man he always was, to put all his armor back on—and to never breathe a word of this night again to anyone. He had too many enemies, both in the Realms and on Earth.

Truly falling for a woman was tantamount to drawing a target on her back.

And yet, he'd risk it all to feel like that again with her.

ANDI LAY UNDER HIM, wrecked for the second—or fourth! But who was counting?—time that night, breathing heavy, feeling the weight of him on top of her, the heat flowing off of him everywhere that they matched. The temptation to grab hold of him and not let go was *so* strong.

But she found it in her somewhere and squirmed beneath him instead. He took the hint, making an acquiescing noise before brushing her lips with a kiss, then moving back to his own seat, reaching down to pull his jeans on.

That—*they*—had been something else. Ever since they'd started fucking. Oh God, she'd known in the restaurant that it was good, but this time with him here, it was deeper somehow—like they were connected, almost.

And it'd been *so* much less safe.

She knew she couldn't love him yet, both because that was *silly* and she was abso-fucking-lutely not letting herself fall for someone so quickly. She was too smart for that, and she was *not* her mom. And besides, Andi never could just relax. She had plenty of other friends who could—who got to daydream about stupid things without feeling foolish—who could test their boundaries and entertain unsafe things. But Andi was always the watchdog—the natural golden retriever of any group—the girl who knew where all her girlfriends were at the club and how likely they were to puke on the way home and if they needed to be navigated away from any decisions they'd regret come morning.

How the hell had she let all that slide for him? It wasn't the money, and it wasn't the dragon. He just *fit* her. It was the only way she could explain it. It felt like she was supposed to be with him, and she'd been feeling like that ever since the other night—fighting it, even, if she were honest with herself.

Fast forward to tonight—in that final moment when he'd been inside her—when she'd felt everything *so much more,* and she knew he had too. She'd seen it in his eyes and felt it in his body; it radiated off of him the same as his heat had.

God, she was falling for him!

Andi bit her lips and swallowed. No, no, no. *No!* Absolutely not. Just because she wanted to let go and lose control, it didn't mean she wanted to lose her heart.

But she'd never, ever, felt like that with Josh.

She watched him pull his jeans on—breathless and afraid. Andi Ngo did not catch feelings. Not like this. And she'd already opened herself up to him once tonight and been rebuffed. Nothing had changed! Not in their circumstances or in their surroundings! Every magically chiseled inch of his body glowed by the dashboard lights as if he aimed to prove her point. He was still a rich playboy who could become a dragon, and she—what was she? A passing fancy? A fuck buddy? Just some friend? No matter what he'd said earlier or how good the words made her feel, he had all the reasons in the world to leave her again.

And the gold coin his friend had given him swung in her peripheral vision, still rocking from their final round of thrusts. From the way Damian hadn't wanted to talk about things earlier, she was certain his friend had been killed in action. And she knew in the pit of her stomach, sinking deeper all the time, that after everything she'd seen tonight—even if he didn't *want* to leave her—eventually, he would. *Death was death, right?* For her own good, if nothing else. Just like he'd tried to in the restaurant.

Andi swallowed. She knew herself—her soul—couldn't handle him flipping another switch, and there was no way she could live happily ever after waiting for a blow to land.

There was only one way to not get hurt. Get out in front of it.

Acknowledge things and then close the book. No dog-ears, no bookmarks.

She arranged her coat around herself before she began because this was a conversation better not had naked. "Okay, so," she said, steeling herself. "Thank you so much for an interesting evening."

Damian looked over at her from where his hands were redoing his belt buckle, and he blinked. "Excuse me?"

Stay strong. You tell people bad news all the time at work. You're used to people being disappointed in you.

"I said, thank you for an interesting evening, Mr. Blackwood."

His whole body tensed across from her, and he spoke next like he wasn't sure he'd heard her. "You're joking, right, princess?"

The way he said it twisted a knife into her heart. If it hurt this much now, it was confirmation that it was better to get out now while she could.

"If you could please finish taking me home." She fastened the bottom of her coat and zipped it up primly.

Damian stared at her, and she didn't dare match his gaze. It was like there was a livewire between them and he was charging it while she kept trying to let go, but she couldn't, not for as long as he kept electrifying her. "I wish things were different," he said, his voice dark. Andi swallowed again, fighting not to sway.

She really didn't owe him any other explanation, except for the look on his face that said she was breaking some deep part inside of him. "You said it yourself at the restaurant—and in here, just an hour ago. You're a jerk, and you're dangerous. And as good as I am at dating assholes, apparently, I'm not willing to go there again. Not even for you." She found strength in her as the words kept tumbling out, knowing that if she was going to cut the cord between them, she was would have to be cruel.

He weighed her words, and she watched his jaw work as his teeth ground before saying, "I'm not like the others," in a growl. Pre-dawn light poured through the windows and over his face and he looked so stricken then, this massive man brought low, and Andi realized she knew the exact right thing to say to end it—even if it killed her.

"Really?" she snorted softly. "Because I have a hundred-dollar bill that says otherwise."

He took a big gulp of air as if he'd been gut punched and swallowed, but he didn't say another word as he twisted back to the steering wheel to turn on the car.

Damian focused on the road ahead in silence. The ache in his chest was from the night's exertions, he told himself, just a reminder that he needed to get back to training harder, rather than wasting his time with humans. She knew who he was, what he was, and he had gotten exactly what he wanted.

Her acknowledgement that together, they were a bad idea.

Even though he wanted her more than he'd wanted anything ever before in his life.

Lust raced through him like wildfire—he knew how good they'd been, and he needed it again—but instead of yanking the car over, he wrung the steering wheel until his knuckles were white, forcing himself to stay on the road.

Damian glanced over at her and saw her staring straight ahead, completely resigned. It was like a wall had come down between them.

Fly over it! his dragon suggested, intensely concerned.

He swallowed as his pride raged inside himself, not knowing what to do. He shouldn't have to explain himself. He should just get what he wanted at all times; it was what he deserved—and that kind of thinking was why he'd left the Realms. If he'd really wanted to be an asshole, he could just go back there and be king.

He wheeled his car into the lot in front of her apartment, parked, and started talking before she could reach for the door handle. "My people are working on technology to predict when the gates will open, so we can get to them faster and close them in time."

Andi looked at her hands in her lap instead of him. "I'm not sure I know what you're trying to say."

He searched desperately for any kindness in her tone. "That I won't always have to be dangerous."

She looked at him then, her brown eyes dark like wet stone and every bit as unforgiving. "No? So...just a jerk, then?"

"Andi," he said, his voice low. "I was trying to keep you safe."

Her smile was bright and brittle. "And you did. Congratulations. You were right. You are dangerous to people who might care," she said.

And he knew she wasn't talking about the monsters.

He had hurt her.

"Most people have to work themselves up to that caliber of... dangerousness. It takes a lot of practice, but no, you...Olympic level, right off the bat."

The thought of anyone else hurting her—especially other men—made him murderous, no matter that he was among their number. He inhaled deeply so as not to yell, and the air still smelled like her—apples, saltwater, caramel.

"But...we...just..." he said slowly, spreading his hands wide, indicating the space in the car they'd occupied, their bodies entwined. Her hair was spread over her shoulders and the blue streak followed a line he'd kissed from her throat to her breast.

"Olympic level too, yeah," Andi granted. "But, Damian, I'm telling you no."

And it felt like the first time he'd really heard it. Maybe in his entire life. Suddenly there wasn't enough air for both of them inside the car, and inside of him, his dragon was roiling just like his stomach. "No?" he asked her louder than he'd meant.

"It's not just my last name," she said, shaking her head at him.

But he knew that that wasn't really how one was supposed to say her name. She was telling him the family name given to clueless outsiders, the name given to those to who couldn't be bothered to learn the difference.

She was telling him he wasn't anything to her.

And it hurt.

He watched her try to hide herself with her coat beside him, divorced from emotion. He would feel it all later, in a rush, but if he let himself feel it now with her still so close...maybe she was right. Maybe he would always be dangerous.

But goddammit, he did not want it to end with her like this.

"Here," he said, his voice guttural, handing his coat over. She took it from him and used it like a sarong, kicking out of the last of her dress.

"Thanks," she said when she was done. "I'm going to go now." He watched her inhale as she chose her next words carefully. "I don't regret a thing."

She swung her door open as he swung his, too, stepping out, even though he didn't know what to say or do to change her mind. "This isn't the end, Andi."

He didn't shout, but he projected his voice loud enough for her to hear. She didn't turn around. She just kept walking—away from him.

Go to her! his dragon commanded. *Now!* It wrestled with him, fighting him for control in a blind rage, and he wanted with all his soul to let it win, but he choked it back.

We can't! This...is for the best, he told his dragon, adding, *for now,* to calm it.

Because it was true. There was no way he was going through the rest of his life without her. Whatever he had to do to make her trust him again, to make her feel safe around him, he would get it done. He watched her ass sway as she started up the stairs to her apartment, and then saw her stop on the final one to look back at him.

She was fierce and beautiful, and she was his, and there was no way in hell this was over.

***

Thank you for reading DRAGON CALLED! Andi and Damian's

story isn't over yet! Turn the page for an exclusive excerpt from DRAGON DESTINED!

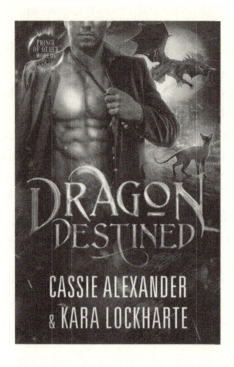

Find out what happens when Andi discovers dangerous magic threatening patients at her hospital.

What's a mortal nurse to do, other than call on the most magical being she knows, even if he is hazardous to her heart?

EXCERPT FROM DRAGON DESTINED

Her chest heaved with the force of her confession, her cheeks flushed red, and her gaze cast down as if she were afraid to meet his eyes. He caught her chin and made her look at him.

"But you are strong, Andi. In ways that you can't even see." His mate had the room for the whole world inside her heart, and she longed to always do the right thing, no matter what it cost her. How rare was that in this day and age? How dangerous was her drive to be good? "But that doesn't matter now," he whispered, his voice husky.

She frowned at him, her brow furrowing over her dark eyes. "Why?"

"Because I'm not leaving you until you push me away."

He watched his words hit her like hard rain, making her flinch—not because she was scared of him, he knew, but because she was frightened of his kindness. She bit her lips, and her gaze went distant as her breathing sped up, and he knew she was thinking about what he'd said, trying to decide if he truly meant it, letting his words echo in her mind. He hoped that there they would multiply, filling in all the gouges left on her by other people's cruel abandonments, that the first sharp pain would dull into a warm and roaring downpour that left her satisfied.

I'm not leaving you, I'm not, I'm not, he thought in time with his own heartbeat, willing for her to hear it again.

If he hadn't still had her chin in his hand, he never would've known. But he felt it then, a slight nod, as her mind returned from wherever it had been, judging him against her past, back to being fully present. And then she bowed her head to kiss the hand that held her.

A rumble erupted out of him, the sound of everything that he'd been keeping caged. He picked her up and pulled her over him, her kicking out of the bottom of her dress on the way, before he splayed her across his still clothed lap, her in nothing but her underwear. He took one of her thighs in each hand and rubbed her against his cock beneath the denim of his jeans, arching up against her.

"Yes," she whispered, "please," she begged and reached down between her legs to work the buckle of his belt.

Continue reading Andi and Damian's story in DRAGON DESTINED!

EXCERPT FROM DRAGON DESTINED

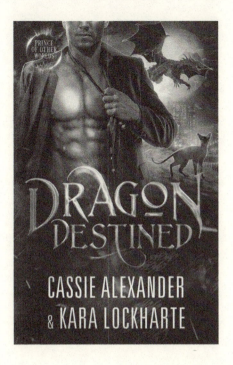

And if you want exclusive access to the Andi and Damian prequel story, *Dragons Don't Date*, in ebook and audio, join Cassie's newsletter!

ALSO BY CASSIE ALEXANDER

PRINCE OF THE OTHER WORLDS (co-written with Kara Lockharte)

(Andi & Damian's story)

Dragon Called

Dragon Destined

Dragon Fated

Dragon Mated

WARDENS OF THE OTHER WORLDS (co-written with Kara Lockharte)

(each book is a standalone)

Dragon's Captive (Sammy & Rax)

Wolf's Princess (Austin & Ryana)

Wolf's Rogue (Zach & Stella)

Dragon's Flame (Tarian & Seris)

…and don't forget to join Cassie's newsletter for access to an exclusive Andi and Damian prequel story, *Dragons Don't Date*, plus *Bewitched*, a Jamison and Mills novella!

THE DARK INK TATTOO SERIES

Blood of the Pack

Blood at Dusk

Blood by Moonlight

Blood by Midnight

Blood at Dawn

Cassie's Stand Alone Books

The House: Come Find Your Fantasy -- a choose your own adventure erotica

Rough Ghost Lover

Her Future Vampire Lover

Her Ex-boyfriend's Werewolf Lover

The Edie Spence Urban Fantasy Series

Nightshifted

Moonshifted

Shapeshifted

Deadshifted

Bloodshifted

Sign up for more news from Cassie here!

Also by Kara Lockharte

Dragon Lovers

Betrothed to the Dragon

Belonging to the Dragon

Bonded to the Dragon

Dragon Lovers Complete Vol. 1

The Space Shifter Chronicles

(Science Fiction Romances)

NOVELS

Wanted by the Werewolf Prince

Taken by the Tigerlord

Desired by the Dragon King (coming soon)

SHORT STORIES

The Boy Who Came Back a Wolf (free to newsletter subscribers)

The Lady and the Tigershifter

In Search of Skye

Made in United States
North Haven, CT
29 September 2024

57998891R00136